# DREAMERS AND MISFITS

## OF MONTCLAIR

# DREAMERS AND MISFITS
# OF MONTCLAIR

## MARK PATERSON

Publishers of Singular
Fiction, Poetry, Nonfiction, Translation, Drama and Graphic Books

Library and Archives Canada Cataloguing in Publication

Title: Dreamers and misfits of Montclair / Mark Paterson.
Names: Paterson, Mark, 1971- author.
Description: Short stories.
Identifiers: Canadiana (print) 20190131985 | Canadiana (ebook) 20190131993 |
    ISBN 9781550968361 (softcover) | ISBN 9781550968378 (EPUB) |
    ISBN 9781550968385 (Kindle) | ISBN 9781550968408 (PDF)
Classification: LCC PS8631.A832 D74 2019 | DDC C813/.6—dc23

Copyright © Mark Paterson, 2019
Cover art by Marc Tessier
Book designed by Michael Callaghan
Typeset in Big Caslon and Birka fonts at Moons of Jupiter Studios
Published by Exile Editions Ltd ~ www.ExileEditions.com
144483 Southgate Road 14 – GD, Holstein, Ontario, N0G 2A0
Printed and Bound in Canada by Marquis

We gratefully acknowledge the Canada Council for the Arts, the Government of Canada, the Ontario Arts Council, and the Ontario Media Development Corporation for their support toward our publishing activities.

Conseil des Arts   Canada Council
du Canada          for the Arts

Canadä

ONTARIO ARTS COUNCIL
CONSEIL DES ARTS DE L'ONTARIO
an Ontario government agency
un organisme du gouvernement de l'Ontario

Ontario
Ontario Media Development
Corporation

Canadian sales representation: The Canadian Manda Group, 664 Annette Street, Toronto ON M6S 2C8 www.mandagroup.com 416 516 0911

North American and international distribution, and U.S. sales: Independent Publishers Group, 814 North Franklin Street, Chicago IL 60610 www.ipgbook.com toll free: 1 800 888 4741

This book is for Lynn Brown

Later they will come to realize that for a few moments they believed in something extraordinary, & will perhaps be driven as a result to seek out some more intense mode of existence.

—HAKIM BEY, *T.A.Z.*:
*The Temporary Autonomous Zone,*
*Ontological Anarchy, Poetic Terrorism*

# SALUT KING KONG

The summer that I was sixteen, I got a call from my friend Dave Greenwood. The people two houses from his were having a garage sale. There was a gorilla costume. Dave knew I'd be interested.

I couldn't find my shoes. My dad's running shoes were in the vestibule, idle. He called them tennis shoes but he didn't play tennis. Or, for that matter, run. What did he even need shoes for anyway, on a Saturday? My feet were smaller than his so, as I ran to Chapleau Street, I had to stretch out my toes and point them against the insides of the soles to keep the shoes from flopping off my feet.

The gorilla suit was stuffed inside a worn-out cardboard box. The costume came in six parts: a mask with a rubber face surrounded by black fake fur, two hands and two feet (also combinations of rubber and fur), and a bulky, furry body with a Velcro zipper strip up the back. It was perfect. I gladly handed over seventy dollars for the thing, money I'd earned sweating over the grill at the local McDonald's. I went home, kicked my father's shoes off, and tried the gorilla costume on.

Then I took a walk along the main street of town.

The suit was hot and scratchy. There was a rank, industrial scent inside the mask. My eyes didn't line up perfectly with the eyeholes so I had to pull down slightly on the nose to see properly. I'd never felt so vibrant in all my life.

Traffic slowed on Sir-Wilfrid-Laurier Boulevard. Horns tooted. Hands waved at me from rolled-down windows. A few people on foot, particularly people walking dogs, crossed to the other side of the street, but most were amused and friendly. "Salut King Kong!" a grand-fatherly type quipped, pleased with himself. He was smoking and I motioned at his cigarette with my fake simian hand, brought two furry fingers to my lips and mimed puffing. The man produced a pack of Player's Light from his front shirt pocket. He cocked his head and carefully threaded a cigarette through my mask's mouth opening. Then he lit it for me. "Merci," I grunted, the way I imagined a talking gorilla might. Smoke filled the inside of the mask, stinging my eyes.

I walked a few more blocks and came to the intersection of Sir-Wilfrid-Laurier and Curé-Antoine-Labelle. Everybody called this juncture The Four Corners; a gas station on each of them except the one where The Montclair Inn stood, long-standing haven of career and underage drinkers alike. It was known simply as The Inn, though those two words did not appear anywhere on the beige stucco building. The large neon sign affixed to the edge of the roof read, in red block letters, MONTCLAIR; our town's unofficial welcome sign with (noticeable only at night) a burnt-out T.

I had a nightmare when I was five. A triceratops was charging through Montclair, trampling everything in its path. People fled as cars, houses, the gas stations at The Four Corners, The Inn, everything, was flattened. It was the one dream from childhood that stayed with me over the years.

The McDonald's where I worked was across the street and a couple of doors down from The Inn. They had recently installed a security camera in the drive-through, trained on the microphone where customers gave their orders from their cars. Inside, we couldn't keep our eyes off the screen, thrilling at the sight of familiar faces on (sort of) TV. "There's my History teacher!"

I knew Theresa Black was working and I knew she was probably working in the drive-through – she always did. I made my way toward the microphone amid the cheers, shouts and honking horns in the parking lot. I waved my furry hand to the camera under the roof over-hang. As one car advanced, and before the next one pulled up, I put my rubber gorilla nose to the microphone grill and grunted, "Milkshake. Chocolate. And fries. To dip in the milkshake."

"Tim?"

A few weeks before, when we had the staff room to ourselves, I'd revealed to Theresa my private fondness for French fries dipped in chocolate milkshake. It sounds disgusting, and it did to Theresa, but there's something in that combination of salt, grease, hot potato, and cold, sweet chocolate ice cream. After some coaxing, I got her to try. She wasn't crazy about it but did concede it was not as gross as she'd expected it to be.

Since then, on days when our shifts coincided, we'd been coordi-nating our breaks. We employed affected nonchalance, like it didn't really matter if I could get away from the kitchen at the very same time that she could leave the drive-through, pretending it was a happy but unimportant coincidence. My somersaulting stomach and hot ear-lobes were not as blasé about it.

I made my way around to the other side of the McDonald's, wav-ing to customers waiting in line in their cars. Theresa was leaning out the pickup window. Her dark bangs curled like a little wave beneath the brim of her green McDonald's cap. The skin on the upper regions of her cheeks was shiny with the grease of a four-hour shift. "Tim? Is that really you?" She was beaming.

"It's me," I replied, nearing the window. "I forgot to shave."

"You're crazy." She slipped me a milkshake. "I'm finishing in ten minutes?"

Fuck the casual act, I thought. "That's great! I'll be in the park."

"I'll bring fries," Theresa said. "Now go, I gotta work."

In the park behind the McDonald's I sat atop an orange picnic table with my feet up on the bench. I pulled the gorilla mask off and basked in the breeze cooling my sweaty face. I took a long drink of milkshake through my straw. From my spot I could see, beside the McDonald's, the back of the Harvey's, and beside that the back of Buffet Chinois Ben Foo. Across the street from the Chinese place was the Tim Hortons and beside it was the Provi-soir. Next, in the direction of The Four Corners, was The Montclair Inn. For the better part of a year, I'd been thinking about my old triceratops nightmare a lot, and how I really wouldn't mind, would in fact like, for something to come along and raze this lifeless town to the ground. Wipe it off the map. If not a dinosaur, a giant ape could do the job, and nicely. Salut King Kong, the place is all yours.

But in that moment, sweating in my new gorilla costume in the park, I had other things on my mind. There'd be more garage sales to scope out next weekend. Dave had his licence now and we had plans to go see Fugazi in Montreal in August. Chocolate milkshakes were awesome. I loved Theresa Black and, in just a few minutes, she was meeting me in the park.

# THE DAD WAS DRINKING

The dad was drinking but only the dad knew about it so, in the middle of the night, when the kid's cough became loud and unnerving, resembling a seal's bark, it was only normal for the mom to ask the dad to take the kid out for a drive.

"With the window open a bit. To let her breathe the cold air." The mom was suddenly overcome by a sneeze. Her head recoiled with the force of it. She wiped her nose with a ball of crumpled tissue in her fist. Her eyelids looked heavy, had for a few days, and her nostrils and lips were chapped. "Info-Santé said you jack the heat. And cover her with blankets. I'd do it, but—" The mom stopped as another sneeze struck. She shrugged her shoulders, wiped at her nose again, and sniffed loudly.

The dad pretended to have to go to the bathroom and left the mom to dress the kid in her snowsuit. He sat on the toilet seat and put his face in his hands and thought about the kid's small hands and how difficult it was to get them inside mittens, and he fell asleep.

The dad woke to tapping on his shoulder. "Come on," the mom said. "She's ready now."

The dad had been a dad for nearly eighteen months. After the kid was born, he learned how to change a diaper and how to warm a bottle and how to sit the kid on his lap, support her gently by the chin, and pat her on the back until she burped. He learned the secret to solving the puzzle of buttons on a onesie was to always begin with the very bottom snap, down along the foot. He learned to leave new bottles of gin in the trunk of his car until the mom was asleep. He learned to alleviate his hangovers - with varying success - with Sausage McMuffins, medium black coffees, and short naps in the car before work.

What the dad liked to do at night while the mom and the kid slept upstairs was drink gin and Sprite on the couch with the lights out and watch art-house movies on his laptop with his headphones on. The dad was a quiet and undemanding drunk.

The kid was sitting on the floor in front of the vestibule doorway, looking inflated and immobile in her snowsuit. She coughed her terrible seal bark and cried a little and barked again. The mom crouched down beside the kid and stroked her head while speaking quiet and comforting words. The dad stepped around them elegantly and put on his jacket and gloves. "You better wear a tuque," the mom said. "It's going to be cold in the car." The dad pretended this was all perfectly comprehensible.

He opened the front door to blowing snow. The snow appeared, somehow, to be falling upward. For an astonished moment, the dad observed the scene. Then he surmised it was only the wind whipping snow up from where it had collected on the front porch. "It's just the wind," he told the mom in a serious manner. "It's just whipping snow up from the porch."

"Okay, um, thanks for the weather update." The mom laughed a little at her own joke. The dad took the mom's laughter as a cue to laugh, too. Then the mom coughed and the dad stopped laughing.

Outside, he slogged through the snow from the front door to the driveway, not really lifting his feet at all. He started the car and blasted the heat. The mom opened the back door and deposited the kid into the car seat. "Thank you for making that path," she sang. The dad understood she was talking to him and he understood the juvenile intonation was for the kid's benefit but he had no idea what the mom was talking about.

Once the kid was strapped in, the mom closed the back door and backed away. The dad put the car into reverse. The mom jumped up and down and waved her arms like she was signalling to an airplane overhead. The dad put the car into park again. The mom approached the dad's window. "You have to open her window a bit!" She mimed rolling down a car window, cranking the air with one closed fist. "She has to breathe the cold air. To open her airway." Her voice was muffled on the other side of the glass. The dad saluted and cracked open the kid's window with a button on the driver's side control panel.

As he drove away from the house, the dad summoned all of his powers of concentration. Still he gunned the gas pedal and, in an attempt to compensate, hit the brakes too hard. His stomach cramped. He felt a sweat form on his brow. He glanced back at the house. The mom was still in the driveway, waving goodbye. Tentatively, the dad tried the gas pedal again. He found the right pressure, and he was off. He tapped gently at the brake as he approached a stop sign. The snowy streets were deserted but he was careful to make a full stop and, at the same time, not to stop for a suspiciously long time. It was a delicate balance.

The kid coughed in the back seat. The dad tilted the rear-view mirror and looked at her. Only her little eyes, nose and mouth were visible amid the bundle of tuque, scarf and blankets the mom had made. They drove beneath a streetlamp and the car's interior was briefly illuminated. In that moment, the kid's eyes met the dad's in the mirror and the dad thought he saw the kid smile a little. When they passed under the next lamp the dad said, "Peekaboo." The kid laughed but it sounded like a seal bark and the dad didn't do anything special at the streetlamp after that.

The dad felt hungry. He drove toward the strip mall. He wanted Sweet Chili Heat Doritos. The digital clock on the car radio read 2:57. *Please let the dépanneur be open,* the dad thought. *Let it be open and*

*I'll never drink again.* He pulled into the parking lot and carefully coasted to a stop. The lights inside the dépanneur were dim. He could just make out the potato chip display and the magazine rack. He'd known all along the dépanneur would be closed but he felt like he'd tried anyway.

The strip mall was in the upper part of town. The parking lot stretched to the edge of a hill that overlooked the autoroute. The dad aimed the car toward the end of the parking lot and the tall snowbanks built up over the winter by the snowplows. He drove to a V-shaped opening between two snowbanks and stopped, facing the gap. He put the car into park, leaving the engine running. Just to be sure, he looked at the shifter and said, "You are in park." A smile formed on his lips. He jabbed one finger into the centre of his chest. "And you," he said, "are intoxicated."

The dad stared through the windshield, the wipers sweeping intermittently. The skyline of Montreal made up a small section of the distant horizon. The buildings downtown, shimmering with electric light, looked about as tall as the dad's forefinger. Domed St. Joseph's Oratory, nestled on the slope of Mount Royal to the right of the city centre, could be blotted out – if he closed one eye – by his thumb. He thought what a fun thing hiding buildings behind his thumb would be in the spring, with the weather warmer, and the kid a little older.

The dad woke to tapping on the driver's side window. It was the mom, bundled up, clutching herself out in the cold of the parking lot, illuminated by the headlights of her own car. The dad's car's engine was still running, the heat still blasting, and the clock read 4:02. He unlocked the doors with a button on the driver's side control panel while attempting to do the math in his head. The mom climbed into the back seat next to the kid. The dad knew it had been at least an hour but he couldn't keep the numbers straight enough to get an accurate measure. In the rear-view mirror he watched the mom fuss with the blankets and the scarf. She put her ear near the kid's face. "Oh," the mom said. "Her breathing's much better." The dad felt the mom's hand on his head. She was patting it. "Nice job. You're such a good dad."

# WHAT HAVE YOU DONE?

## KEITH'S GUM

The first week of school, we dressed in our summer clothes and the teachers kept all of the windows open. An easygoing feeling prevailed thanks to the spillover of hot August weather. We laughed easier, lunched on dépanneur junk food, and went to class casually late – close enough to the bell that we avoided trouble for the most part, but long enough after its ringing to feel a slight measure of freedom, of power. While the weather had something to do with it, I think the main reason for the blithe mood was the fact that we were *older*, finally starting our last year of high school. On the Friday night, we capped off that first week of school by going to see *Aliens*.

The movie theatre was in a building unto itself in the vast parking lot of Carrefour Laval. Terry Stahl's mom drove right up to the front entrance and, as the car idled in the fire lane, she warned Terry – and, by extension, us – not to make her wait once the movie was over. She was going shopping, but the mall would close before the end of the movie. Irritation coloured her voice. "I'm looking at twenty, maybe thirty minutes with nothing to do."

We got out of the car and Terry's mom drove away. We took turns parroting her last line in exaggerated, high-pitched voices.

Keith Porter was waiting for us inside; his dad had dropped him off at the movie theatre, straight from Keith's swim team practice. Keith had his learner's permit and he was excited to announce he'd done the driving. "Eleven kilometres," he reported. "Mostly autoroute."

Of all the people I knew, only Keith would have noted the distance of the drive. We really gave it to him for that.

It was dark by the time we went back outside after the movie. There was a line of cars in the fire lane with their headlights on. We found Terry's mom and guys started climbing into the car. I was still out on the sidewalk when we realized there wasn't room for everyone. Keith's presence hadn't been accounted for. He ducked his head to speak through the passenger-side window. "I'll call my dad."

"I can't just leave you alone," Terry's mom said.

"I could stay with him," I volunteered.

"Do you need a quarter?"

After Keith got off the payphone, he looked at his watch. "We've got half an hour. Let's explore."

I could not imagine saying something like *Let's explore*. Especially to someone my own age. I was too careful, too guarded, to expose myself to the ridicule such a statement might prompt. Keith, however, had no filter for corny, enthusiastic statements. We teased him for it, called him The Cheese Factory, but he never acted like it bothered him. Comfort in his own skin was Keith's greatest strength. I could never tell him, but I envied him for that.

I allowed *Let's explore* to pass without comment. Being alone with Keith, what would have been the point?

With the mall closed for the night, we headed for the Sheraton, which was also located in the parking lot, a few steps from the theatre. A pair of automatic glass doors opened to a brightly lit hotel lobby of leather couches, chairs, and plastic plants. A wide, dark red carpet led to the front desk. Off to one side was a stand that sold snacks, post-cards, and other small items. There was a wide jar filled with cigars, each individually wrapped in transparent plastic. A round orange sticker on the jar said 50 cents. I was a quarter short but Keith covered me.

We took our cigars outside. Keith unwrapped his and wedged it in the corner of his mouth. He flashed me the resulting open-mouth smile. We walked to the edge of the parking lot, where the concrete gave way to weedy grass. A short slope led down to a long chain-link fence that separated the parking lot from the autoroute. On the other side, cars and trucks sped north and south. It felt like we were hidden away – too low down in the grade to be seen from the parking lot, too insignificant to be noticed by anyone passing by on the autoroute. It was still warm out. We lit the cigars. I inhaled little gulps of smoke. It was pungent and I coughed a little and I felt buzzed.

Keith took short drags on his cigar, making kissing sounds. His ember flashed red like the taillights on the other side of the fence.

"Do you remember that gum I swallowed on my ninth birthday?"

I had been friends with Keith since kindergarten. I had probably gone to all of his birthday parties when we were in elementary school. One year there was a round cake with white icing, decorated with red gumballs in the shape of the number nine. The dye from the gumballs had seeped into the icing, forming little puddles of pink. After blowing out his candles, Keith had plucked one of the gumballs from the cake and popped it into his mouth. His mother was cutting pieces of cake and passing them around the table on paper plates. Keith announced he was going to swallow his gum. His mother asked him if he had shit in his brain – Mrs. Porter was the funniest; she swore unapologetically in front of kids. A chorus of laughter erupted all around the table. Keith bobbed his head like a chicken and swallowed.

I told him I remembered the gum. "What about it?"

Keith flicked cigar ash onto the grass. "Seven years is nearly up. My birthday's in two weeks. It's almost out of my system now."

I smiled, recalling the rest – really the beginning – of the story. Not long before Keith's ninth birthday party, at school, a kid named Patrick

Lamontagne had been caught chewing gum in class. Patrick was a year older than the rest of us because he had failed a grade. He was persistently in trouble. He was once suspended a whole week for selling torn-out pages of his father's *Penthouse* magazines for 25 cents apiece.

Mrs. Woods told Patrick to throw out his gum, but he swallowed it, claiming he'd never had any. Without missing a beat, Mrs. Woods said, "Oh, good. Because for a second there I thought you'd swallowed it. Gum takes seven years to digest, you know. It just sits there in your stomach. For seven years."

Our teacher was trying to scare him, but Patrick had only snickered, saying, "That's so cool."

Keith kissed at his cigar. "It's weird," he said between puffs, patting his stomach, "I'm sort of, like, sad that it's nearly all gone."

I thought it was just a myth, that gum takes seven years to digest, and I was about to say as much, but I stopped myself. Keith had been waiting for this moment nearly half his life. I didn't want to rob him of it.

We stomped out our cigars and walked back to the movie theatre to wait for Keith's dad. When he arrived, he got out of the car and handed the keys to Keith. I slid into the back seat, feeling stupid for not having my own learner's permit yet. I watched Keith prepare, meticulously, to drive. He fastened his seatbelt, adjusted the rear-view mirror, checked the side mirrors (he announced he was doing this), started the engine, and turned the headlights on. He signalled, and the car began to move.

A couple of times before leaving the parking lot, right after stop signs, his dad said, "Try not to rev it so much."

But Keith could drive. My envy only grew.

On the autoroute, his dad told us we smelled like cheap cigars.

"*Very* cheap," Keith replied.

I saw the back of Mr. Porter's head quiver and I heard him chuckle. I was amazed he wasn't angry. From the glove compartment, he produced a pack of Dentyne. He held out a piece for Keith. "Your mother won't be very happy with you if you come home smelling like that."

Without turning around, he reached back over his shoulder with a piece for me. "And you, Joey? I don't suppose yours will be pleased, either."

I took the gum and muttered thank you. The rest of the ride was quiet. Mr. Porter must have checked the blind spot out the passenger window a hundred times between the mall and my house.

## NATALIE ST-ONGE

I signed myself up for a driving course that October. It started with theory classes, given once a week at the driving school in a big room with plain, white walls and grey industrial carpeting. The class was made up almost entirely of kids from school, all jammed into the one autumn session offered in English. The teacher, Vincent, could speak English well enough but he liked to tell jokes in French. Half the class would laugh politely or groan. The other half, which included me, barely understood a word.

There was a dépanneur across the street from the driving school and we flocked there during the ten-minute break Vincent gave us halfway through class. Chocolate bars and chips and Cokes. Some of the kids, the rockers especially, smoked cigarettes out on the sidewalk during the break. They looked rough with their long hair, jean jackets, and Kodiak boots, but I had known some of them for so long that I could recall very clearly what they had looked like two feet shorter, wearing soccer uniforms and sporting bowl haircuts.

Natalie St-Onge was in the driving class. She went to my high school but I only knew her enough to say hi. She had dark hair and dark eyes and a pouty bottom lip. She had a little mole on the edge of her cheekbone and, if you looked past the layer of foundation she wore, a forehead full of acne. She owned at least twenty wool sweaters, different colours and patterns. She had a job at the Burger King. I'd had a crush on Natalie St-Onge for so long it was hard to remember what it felt like to not have one.

The second week of driving class, during the break outside the dépanneur, I decided to stand near Natalie. As close as I could get without being obvious. Or creepy. She was talking to a friend. I stood right next to her, but at a casual angle. My heart was beating so fast.

Natalie had a pack of Thrills. She shook out a piece. My head turned slightly toward the sound of the gum rattling inside the box. "You want one?" she offered. "They taste like soap."

I felt flushed. I couldn't manage a response. I just stood there. Natalie reached out and grasped my wrist, firmly but not violently, and turned my palm upwards. She placed a piece of gum in it. I put the gum in my mouth and started to chew. I wasn't sure what soap was supposed to taste like, but I said she was right, it tasted like soap. Her eyes widened and she smiled.

"Weird, eh?"

Totally weird, I replied.

The gum lost its flavour quickly but I chewed it throughout the rest of class, thinking about Natalie's fingers, how they'd touched the gum.

After class, I swallowed it.

The next week, when we went outside on break, I caught up with Natalie again. I asked her to explain a joke Vincent had told in class.

"The one about tea?"

"It was about tea?"

"Don't you know *any* French?"

I shrugged my shoulders.

"You want a gum?"

"Merci."

"You're funny."

When we returned to class Natalie sat in the seat next to mine.

The next day at school, while I was fishing around in my locker, I felt a tap on my shoulder. I turned around. Natalie said hi. She was wearing a baby-blue turtleneck sweater. Her cheeks were tinged red. Two of her friends stepped in and dragged her away, the three of them whispering and stifling laughter.

We started talking on the telephone at night. There were a few moments of silence at first, shy pauses as we sought common ground, things to talk about. I'd clear my throat or say *um* to fill in some of the gaps. Natalie told me about her family – her mother, father, and an older brother. They had a specific arrangement with languages at home. Not rules, just the way things worked. With her mother and brother, she spoke English. With her father, everyone spoke French. I was quiet for a moment as I thought about this. "But what if you're all in the same room? Do you speak English or French?"

"It depends who you're talking to."

"I couldn't imagine talking to one of my parents in another language."

"What do you mean, *another* language?"

I knew exactly what I meant, but I couldn't put it into words. Not, I realized, without sounding completely idiotic.

We took turns describing our friends to each other. A lot of mine had nicknames and I told Natalie the stories behind how they had been acquired. She said The Cheese Factory was a mean name to call Keith. But she laughed as she said it.

I found out Natalie had a whole subset of friends from the French school, who worked with her at the Burger King. I asked her if it was legal for people who were not of royal descent to wear a cardboard Burger King crown. Natalie giggled. I asked her if her manager called the police whenever the Duke of Doubt showed up or if the staff removed him from the premises themselves. I asked her if the Whaler was made with the meat of actual whalers or with the meat of Hartford Whalers. Natalie laughed so loud her mother told her to get off the phone.

"See you at school tomorrow," she said.

"Can't wait," I said, hoping and yet terrified she would read into my reply.

It was quiet on the other end of the line. I thought Natalie had already hung up. But then I heard her speak, quickly and nearly inaudibly.

"Me, too."

And then the line went dead.

## LET'S DRIVE

My father and I had a misunderstanding about driving school: I assumed he'd pay for it and he assumed he could be a dick and still command some amount of respect. When I'd signed up, I told the school I'd bring a cheque the following week. I kept making the same promise, week after week. After four weeks had gone by, Vincent was having no more of it. "You pay next time or you're out."

On Saturday I left the house early. I made my way on foot to the centre of town, The Four Corners. I went into three gas stations and the McDonald's, but it was futile. I could barely string the words together in French to ask for a job application. At the Harvey's the manager was sympathetic, in a powerless sort of way. "If you don't have a lot of French..." He didn't need to complete the thought.

The Burger King was just up the street but I was too humiliated to even try.

For a while I walked aimlessly, passing the pharmacy, the video store, the Pizza Hut, and other businesses where I could not get a job. I had always been terrible in French at school. I could conjugate verbs but I didn't know what half of them meant. Madame Tessier, my Grade Nine French teacher, told me I'd never learn the language. She said I was *bloqué*. It was like a licence to fail. And, thanks to my laziness, it was the only licence I'd have for the foreseeable future.

Outside the hardware store, a familiar car slowed and came to a stop beside me. Two short bursts of the horn drew me closer. Keith was at the wheel of his father's car, alone. I got in.

"You got your licence." I tried to sound happy for him.

"Let's drive," Keith said. His voice was baritone, like he was delivering a big line in a movie. Like he'd been waiting forever to say this to someone. Cheese Factory.

Keith made his way to the autoroute and we headed north. I asked where we were going.

"Somewhere. Anywhere."

We drove for a long time, past Mirabel and Saint-Jérôme, through Prévost. We were in the Laurentians, climbing long rises and gliding down seemingly longer inclines. Going up and down like that was soothing, especially with Keith behind the wheel, smooth and vigilant driver that he was. The mountains rose on either side of us, conifer greens mixed with the oranges, reds, and yellows of changing leaves. A feeling of happy tranquillity was stirring inside of me, its power increasing as the country around us grew wilder. The sky was a crisp, bright blue. There were but a few scattered clouds, high and white.

Keith had Rush playing on the tape deck, the *Permanent Waves* album. I thought how great it must be to just get in a car, put on some music, and go somewhere. Anywhere. The synthesizer parts in "Entre Nous" were so beautiful I knew that if I had been alone, I'd have let myself cry.

Keith exited at Saint-Sauveur. He drove slowly, surveying the unfamiliar landscape. There was a cluster of fast food restaurants and shops not far from the autoroute. Keith pulled into a parking spot near a dépanneur. He turned to me. "Cigar?"

"I'm broke."

"I got it."

We sat on the concrete parking curb in front of Keith's dad's car to smoke. Keith left the car windows down, the tape deck playing loud enough so we could hear. There was only a hint of chill in the air. When I'd woken up that morning, I had no idea I'd be in Saint-Sauveur by noon.

It seemed like there were endless possibilities in the world and the thought made me feel a little sick in the stomach. In a good way.

"Let's talk," Keith said, emulating the same corny tone he'd used when he picked me up. "So. What have you done?"

After some hesitation, I said I had done everything. "With Natalie St-Onge."

"Are you serious?"

"Very."

"Tell me more."

## WHAT HAVE YOU DONE?

The strange thing was, when I told Keith what I told him, it sort of felt like I was telling the truth. Because, I was convinced, it was going to happen. Eventually. So, while one part of my mind was busy fabricating epic sexual exploits, the other was hard at work justifying the lie: my dad wouldn't give me a penny, I couldn't get a job, and I was on the cusp of being kicked out of driving school. I had no control. I decided I deserved something good, a little credit – and more credit than I'd have earned by providing a glowing report about what nice telephone conversations Natalie and I were having. So what if I said we'd done it twice already? What difference did it make, in the grand scheme of things, if the report of the act preceded the act?

It turned out it made a huge difference.

Monday morning at school, the first sign of trouble came courtesy of Terry Stahl. He was waiting for me at my locker. He raised his right arm in the air, offering me a high-five. He nodded his head slowly, in approval of what – at first – I did not know. I hesitated to return the gesture. My friends and I were not the high-fiving types. We often laughed behind the backs of boys who were. Terry wobbled his high-fiving hand. "Come on," he encouraged.

I thought he was fooling around. I gave him a feeble high-five, our palms pressing awkwardly from lack of practice.

"Nice work." Terry's tone was salacious. He raised and dropped his eyebrows in quick succession. He made an O with one hand and stuck the forefinger of the other through it.

I felt queasy. I had asked Keith not to tell anyone. He had assured me he wouldn't. It appeared Terry Stahl was not anyone.

Neither, apparently, was Dean Cousins. "Is it true, Joey?" he asked. Then, in a whisper, "Did you really fuck her?"

My brow felt prickly, my cheeks hot. "Look," I said, "whatever Keith told you guys – it's totally private."

"I certainly *hope* you did it in private," Dean purred, laughing at his own joke. Terry high-fived him.

Just then Keith arrived at the lockers.

"You told these clowns?"

"I wasn't supposed to?"

"I told you not to tell anyone."

"But I was happy for you."

My mind was racing. The guys all looked confused.

The bell rang and I dug into my locker to get my books out. Someone poked me in the back, hard. I turned around. Natalie was standing there with her arms crossed, hugging a textbook to her chest. Her whole face was red. My heart sank. It was like she was trying to hide behind that book. "Did you—?" Natalie cut herself off and glanced at Terry. Then at Dean, then Keith. The looks on their faces. Like little kids with fingers in the pie. Natalie turned to me again. Tears welled in both of her eyes. "What have you done?" Her eyes blinked in quick succession and, as she raised a hand to wipe them, she turned away.

I felt like puking.

I watched Natalie walk away from me and thought about how I would smack the guy in the head who would tell such stories about her.

## THE VOYAGE HOME

During Christmas break, Keith drove a few of us to see the new *Star Trek* movie, *The Voyage Home*. When it was over, we emerged from the theatre to falling snow. On the way back to Keith's car, we ran and slid in our boots on the new snow in the parking lot. We squabbled over who left the longest tracks.

Terry Stahl started in on a William Shatner impersonation, making a case, in Captain Kirk's halting speech pattern, for being the most skilled parking lot slider. The other guys chimed in with Kirk imitations of their own. I had enjoyed the movie. The gloom that had been hovering over me for weeks was still there, but I allowed myself to feel a little bit giddy.

There was a white, two-door hatchback parked near Keith's dad's car. I noticed it because of its radio antenna. It was extremely long; longer than any antenna I'd ever seen. It extended from above the driver's side window to just past the back of the car, drooping from its own weight. It was an obvious modification – no car came with an antenna that long. "Why..." I began, pausing like Shatner would, "does...that car...have...an antenna...the length of...a telephone pole?" The other guys looked where I was pointing and they started to laugh. Terry suggested the car's owner was compensating for something. This elicited another rowdy chorus of laughter.

While Keith brushed the snow from his windows, I made my way over to the white car. I took the end of the antenna in my hand and pulled down on it, feeling the resistance build. I let go. The antenna rapidly sprang back up and reverberated in cartoonish fashion. The other guys were cackling. I was pleased with myself.

From behind us somebody yelled. "Ay!"

It was a short, angry shout, like a dog bark. There were four guys our age, maybe a little older. Bigger than us anyway. Long hair, jean jackets, and Kodiaks. One of them had a moustache. They quickened their pace.

"Get in the car, guys," Keith said nervously. I dashed to his car and we all scrambled inside. I slammed the back door shut.

"Hogues," Terry said from the front passenger seat. We called the rockers at our school *rockers*. We called French rockers *hogues*. I have no idea where the word came from, only that it allowed for distinction.

Keith gunned the engine. His tires spun in place, too fast to gain any traction. The hogues were running toward our car. Without really thinking about it, I started to roll down my window. Keith tried going forward again, slower this time. We started to move. I leaned my head and my two arms out the window and twisted myself to face the hogues as we drove away. I gave them the finger with both hands. Then I rotated my hands inwards, so that both of my extended middle fingers pointed at each other. Then I pointed them both down. And up again. The rage on the hogues' faces was discernible from a good distance.

Keith, ever the professional driver, stopped faithfully at every stop sign on the way out of the parking lot. The hogues, their long antenna bouncing atop the car, were right behind us by the time we merged onto the autoroute.

Their driver was more reckless than ours. They tailgated us. Keith's windshield wipers swept at top speed. Our pursuers' high beams lit up the interior of our car. Keith adjusted his rear-view to cut down on the glare. He looked nervous yet determined. He tried to trick the hogues by signalling for the Sainte-Rose Boulevard exit. He nudged toward it but at the last possible moment veered back onto the autoroute. The hogues were not fooled. They flashed their high beams on and off in mockery.

"Take them into Montclair," I suggested. "We'll lose them on the side streets." I had this notion that familiarity with the territory would somehow put us at an advantage.

As we took the exit, Keith, eyeing the rear-view mirror, said, "Maybe they'll give up."

I could not explain why, but I found myself hoping they would not.

The hogues chased us into Montclair. Keith weaved through street after street, but he could not shake them. At one point, we passed my house. "Could you just drop me off?" I joked. Nobody laughed.

On a curve on Elmwood Street, our tires caught an icy skid. Keith fought the steering wheel but could not regain control. Elmwood turned but the car kept going straight. We left the road to a loud crunching of snow beneath us, the floor vibrating beneath our feet. The snow brought us to a sudden, jolting halt in the middle of someone's front yard.

Two feet from the front bumper, the thick trunk of a tree, branches overhanging and bare, loomed ominously. The snow had stopped us just short of it.

Terry, in the front seat, was the first to say something. "Oh, look. They're coming to help us." I checked the back window. The hogues had pulled up beside the yard. They were exiting their car. Keith said, "Lock the doors."

The hogues beat on the roof of Keith's car. They pounded on the windows with their fists. The one with the moustache trudged through the snow to my side of the car, pointed at me through the window and then spat on it. He began to slam the side of his body against my door.

I sat there, stomach sick with fear, unsure of what would happen next, and thought with no small amount of satisfaction that I had made all of this happen.

# THE BLIND MAN'S HOUSE

There was a little bungalow on Lepage Street that Merry's family always, on their way home from anywhere, drove past. The house had white siding, a blue front door, and blue window shutters. The roof, too, had a hint of blue in it. The small front porch, made of unpainted wooden planks, was barely wider than the front door. Two steps led down to a concrete path that bisected the front lawn. At the edge of the property, growing on either side of the place where the path met with the sidewalk, were two thick rows of rose bushes. When in bloom, their flowers were pink. The house's sole occupant was a blind man.

"There's the blind man's house!" Merry's mother would sing from the front passenger seat as they drove by. If the blind man himself happened to be outside, her voice surged with excitement and the words ran out of her mouth as quickly as she could spew them: "There's the blind man!"

In the back seat, time after time, Merry pressed her forehead to the cold window glass to look. And as their car drove away, she'd scramble to her knees for a glimpse out the back windshield of the blind man tending to his rose bushes, his thin frame encased in a rumpled spring jacket, his exceedingly large and dark glasses, his thick beard and moustache, his head ever so slightly askew.

Sightings of the blind man beyond the immediate vicinity of his property were rare. There was a time in the bank, where Merry was an occasional and reluctant companion of her father's in the interminable line that he waited in on Thursdays after work. The tedium was almost like pain. But that evening there had been a quiet buzz of voices and a collective turning of heads toward the entrance. Merry turned, too, and was thrilled to see the blind man tapping his cane on the floor, aiming himself toward the back of the line, the fingers of his free hand grazing the sloping, grey velvet ropes connecting the polished stanchion posts that led to the tellers' counter. Barely a minute had passed before the bank manager, a small and stocky man in a grey suit, darted from behind the counter, necktie swaying, and strode to the back of the line. After the exchange of a few hushed words, the bank manager led the blind man to a chair in his office.

Merry's father nudged her. "Don't stare," he whispered. Merry wondered what difference it made. She stopped short of asking, however, when she realized her father, along with everyone else in line, was staring at the blind man, rapt. She took advantage of the distraction to reach out and grasp the portion of velvet rope beside her. She gave a good squeeze to what she was forbidden to touch, *not even one finger.*

There was another occasion, with her mother and her older brother, Ted, in the grocery store. They were leaving the produce aisle, Ted riding on the back of the shopping cart and Merry walking alongside it, when their mother suddenly stopped, staring straight ahead. Merry followed her mother's eyes to the meat counter, where the blind man was having a conversation with the butcher. A package of ground beef, held in the butcher's hands, seemed to be the subject of their talk. Merry's mother leaned down so that her head came in line with Merry's. "He's *helping* him," she whispered.

Ted stepped down from his perch on the back of the shopping cart. He placed his fingertips on the edge of the wire basket and mimed piano playing. He shut his eyes tight and tilted his chin upward. He smiled widely and swayed his head, rhythmically, back and forth, in an almost elliptical motion. He'd barely sung one line of Stevie Wonder's "I Just Called to Say I Love You" before Merry punched him, hard, in the kidney.

She spent an hour in her room upon returning home, but Ted's banishment lasted until dinner, and Merry took her punishment without a word of protest.

Over the course of that hour in her room, Merry could think of little else but the blind man. She pictured his face, his glasses, and his beard. In her mind, she saw his house; the rose bushes, the path, and the blue front door. What lay beyond that door, Merry could only speculate. And this she did until her mother told her it was alright to come out of her room again.

"I wonder if the blind man has a TV."

"I'll bet you a million bucks he doesn't," her mother replied.

Merry suggested a person could listen to the TV. She herself had used her tape recorder to capture the sounds of television specials like *It's the Great Pumpkin, Charlie Brown* and *How the Grinch Stole Christmas!* and listened back to them often in her room.

"A radio, I can see," her mother said. "But not a TV. I just don't see what the point would be."

Over time, a picture materialized in Merry's mind of what the interior of the blind man's house might look like: a dark place where curtains remained closed all the time, where light fixtures had no light bulbs screwed into them, and where the mirrors – if there were any – were always dusty. But there would be a TV.

As enjoyable as it was to imagine, Merry craved a glimpse of the real thing.

By the time Merry was fourteen, the blind man had begun to hold less allure for her. Her mother's particular fascination with him never wavered; it was just no longer infectious. The house was still pointed out when they drove by it, but now Merry looked away. She began to think of the blind man as a childhood interest of hers and, therefore, childish. So, in much the same way that she'd relegated certain toys and dolls to storage in the basement furnace room, and in much the same way that certain turns of phrase and jokes out of the mouths of her mother or father made her cringe, Merry tried her best to forget about the blind man.

Her one friend in the world was Edward Lam. Quiet and timid in public, Edward was considerably smaller than the other boys in Grade Nine. A mushroom-shaped clump of hair at the top of his scalp stood perpetually on end. It was customary for boys at Richard Herbert Memorial High School to pat the top of Edward's head (with, often, vicious intensity) as they passed him in the hallways. For Edward, going from class to class was like running a gauntlet.

Merry and Edward spent their lunch hours holed up together in the school library. A massive dictionary lay on a slanted podium. It contained every word imaginable, and countless others they'd never imagined. Anatomy, sex, mental disorders, phobias, names of crimes, methods of torture, profanities – it was all there, tucked in among the ordinary words. All they had to do was find them.

The library had a rack stocked with television show novelizations, dog-eared paperbacks of *Welcome Back, Kotter*; *The Bionic Woman*; *Happy Days*; *The Brady Bunch*; and others. At the centre of each book was a pictorial section containing stills from episodes of the various shows and headshots of the cast members, along with captions. There was something ridiculous about these books, about their very existence, something Merry and Edward both felt but could not readily explain.

The pictures in the books, and, more specifically, the captions, were at the heart of an ongoing collaborative project of theirs. The two were, gradually, methodically, replacing every caption with lines of Adam and the Ants lyrics. Merry had the records, Edward had a typewriter. Merry read the lyrics to Edward over the telephone at night, and Edward would arrive at school the next day with the lines typed on cut-out, thin strips of paper. Over their lunch hour in the library, armed with a glue stick, the pair pasted their caption revisions into the books. Merry loved to gaze at their work, to see pictures of Mr. Kotter and the Sweathogs, Richie Cunningham and the Fonz, and the Brady children juxtaposed with bizarre poetry about Indigenous North Americans, pirates, sex, and Dirk's white socks.

The librarian never so much as glanced at them.

Merry lived within walking distance of school, but several afternoons a week rode Edward's bus to his home with him. His parents owned and operated the Buffet Chinois Ben Foo out on the main street of town. The family lived in a small apartment above the restaurant. Merry and Edward watched MuchMusic and *Degrassi Junior High* on a TV that sat on a folding chair in the living room. They snacked on selections from the buffet, generous portions of whatever happened to be ready: steamed rice, egg rolls, pineapple chicken, beef and broccoli with black bean sauce, spareribs, wonton soup. They had unlimited access to the soda fountain. Merry liked to scoop ice right to the top of a tall plastic glass before pressing the rim of the glass to the lever beneath the red Coke logo to fill it. If she leaned in, the bubbles tickled her face. She'd let the fizz settle in the glass and then fill it some more. Edward liked Sprite.

There was a day when the Coke tasted bland. Edward showed Merry the workings beneath the soda fountain and taught her how to change the empty box of Coke syrup. Edward's mom, passing by with a stack of clean white plates cradled in her arms, said she should come and work at the restaurant when she was a little older. Merry's fingers were left sticky and smelling sweet and she felt a little bit important.

After testing the Coke to Merry's satisfaction, the two left the restaurant and made the ten-minute walk to the Galeries de Montclair shopping mall. The main draw for teenagers was the food court, but

Merry and Edward liked to hang out in front of the Photo Clik. There was a window display offering a view of a white, clinical-looking photo development machine in action. Freshly developed pictures exited the machine via a small conveyor belt and slid along the edge of the window for all to see. Merry and Edward watched the photos go by in sets of twelve, twenty-four, or thirty-six; glimpses of children posing with grandparents, flowers in gardens, birthday parties, cars, families, pets, vacations, and a wide range of out-of-focus shots.

That day, a batch of camping trip pictures slid by behind the window. There were tents, a campfire, a group of young men, and several beer and liquor bottles. There were also rubber masks: Superman, Laurel and Hardy, Groucho Marx, and a horned devil. The men posed for pictures wearing the masks. One of the men wore a long flowered skirt, a long black wig, and shabbily applied clown makeup on his face. He played a tambourine. In one photograph, the devil groped the drag queen clown. In another, Laurel chased Hardy with an axe. Groucho Marx smoked a cigarette through the mouth opening in his mask. Superman wore a wetsuit and flexed his muscles in front of a lake at sunset while, off to the side, Laurel, axe in hand, continued to chase Hardy.

The camping photos gave Merry a thrill, a palpable tingle down the back of her neck. The pictures were funny, even artistic. But beyond their merits, they communicated something to Merry, something she could not put her finger on, except to know that the day had, somehow, been enhanced. That perhaps *she* had been enhanced. There was a fluttering in her stomach. She'd felt like this before – as a child, with a new box of coloured pencils and a pile of blank typing paper laid out on a table, and, more recently, when the idea to sneak Adam and the Ants lyrics into library books struck her – but never with such intensity. She wanted to take photographs of her own. She wanted other people to see her photographs slide by on a conveyor belt in the Photo Clik window. Photographs of what, she didn't know. Not yet. For now, the pure desire to create was a like a cloud, blocking out ideas.

"Do you think I could borrow your parents' camera?"

Edward looked at Merry and raised one eyebrow. "Um, yeah. Sure."

In the last camping photograph that passed by, the drag queen clown stood with hands on knees, mouth agape, a stream of vomit splashing onto the grass.

That evening, at the dinner table, while the rest of the family ate vigorously and noisily, Merry used her fork to push Salisbury steak and mashed potatoes around on her plate. An ear of corn, glistening with melted butter, sat untouched on the plate's edge. She was still stuffed from Edward's buffet, but, feeling her mother's eyes on her, Merry scooped a dollop of mashed potatoes and brought it to her lips. She forced half of what was on her fork into her mouth. She chewed slowly, delayed swallowing.

"Are you feeling alright, Merry?" her mother asked, a little sardonically.

"I'm fine," Merry replied, stuffing the rest of her forkful into her mouth. "I'm just not super hungry tonight."

"You've been eating at that Chinese restaurant again, haven't you?"

Merry shook her head, taking another, larger, bite of mashed potatoes.

"You know what I've told you about eating there, Merry. Bad enough you're ruining your appetite, but Chinese food is full of MSG. It puffs you right up."

Ted giggled with his mouth full. Merry glanced his way. He puffed out his cheeks at her. He had recently taken to calling her "Jabba" every chance he got. Merry had, indeed, been outgrowing her clothes of late, her pants especially. And this despite not getting any taller for some months now. She did her best to hide it from her mother by wearing sweatpants as often as possible, or, when wearing jeans or corduroys, by leaving her pants unbuttoned and wearing an untucked shirt to conceal it. She avoided the mirror in her room and Ted as much as possible; Merry's punches were too slow to catch her brother now.

"Ted's mocking me, Mom."

"We're not talking about Ted right now. We're talking about you. And Chinese food."

"*Ching chong ching*," Ted sang in a high-pitched voice.

"Ted," Merry's father said, trying to conceal a smirk. "Knock it off."

"Mom, I told you: I'm not eating the Chinese food."

"I find that hard to believe. I find that *impossible* to believe. You sit here and you're not even interested in your meal. A *good* meal. You sit here and – you must have noticed it yourself – you're, you're *larger* than you used to be."

"Mom!"

"I'm sorry, but it has to be said. That Chinese restaurant is no good for you. I want you to stay away from it."

"But, Mom!"

"And aren't there some other friends for you to hang around with? Some girls, maybe? Edward's a nice boy, but—"

"But he's a total weirdo," Ted interjected with a satisfied smile.

"And you're a total asshole," Merry shot back before she could stop herself.

Ted cocked his right arm. In his hand, held like a baton, was his gnawed corn cob.

"Ted!" their father shouted. Ted relaxed his arm. "Merry," their father said, turning to her, "watch the language."

They ate without speaking for a few moments, Merry making a real effort to put food in her mouth while her mother watched.

Ted broke the silence. "I saw the blind man at the dépanneur today."

Their mother sat up straighter in her seat. "I wonder what he could have wanted at the dépanneur?"

"Chips?" Merry deadpanned. "Coke, maybe?"

"I've been thinking about something," Ted continued. His fingertips and lips were slick and shiny with melted butter. "If the blind man's blind, why doesn't he have a blind dog?"

"It's called a *Seeing Eye* dog," their mother corrected, pleased with herself.

"Whatever. He doesn't *have* one. He's never had one. How do we even know he's really blind? What if he's faking it? What if he's been faking it all these years? Tricking us."

"Tricking us?" Merry retorted.

"Tricking us into feeling sorry for him."

"Sorry for him?" Merry snapped. "Who feels sorry for him?"

"Well, I certainly do," their mother said, swelling with pride. "I feel sorry for him every time I see him."

"My point is," Ted went on, "he's blind and he doesn't have a blind dog. Isn't that a little strange?"

"You're a little strange."

Ted's corn cob flew end-over-end across the table. It smacked wet against Merry's neck and splatted in her mashed potatoes.

Though she detested him, Merry could have kissed her brother. Not only had he gotten her out of eating the rest of her dinner, he had also provided her with the idea she'd been seeking for her photography project.

Merry went to Edward's again the next day after school. She felt justified in doing so: her mother had not explicitly forbidden her from going. If she were to take her mother's words literally, she had merely said she *wanted* Merry to stay away from the place; she never directly told her not to go. And getting her hands on Edward's camera made any trouble Merry might get into worth it.

She was mindful of leaving room for dinner, and made herself a smaller plate than usual from the buffet, limiting herself to rice, chop suey, and only four spareribs. She poured herself Diet Coke from the soda fountain, hoping Edward wouldn't notice the change. She shuddered at its bitter taste.

Edward's parents kept their camera in the linen closet up in the family's apartment. "They think it's valuable," Edward explained after Merry raised an eyebrow. "They think robbers don't look in linen closets." He pointed to the top shelf. "It's up there. I can't reach it."

The floor inside the closet was crammed with cleaning products, packages of toilet paper, and a vacuum cleaner. Neatly folded towels sat stacked on the first two shelves. The next two shelves held a jumble of discarded restaurant equipment: stainless steel pots and bowls, a spatula with a broken handle, rusty cake pans, and some plastic jugs. Whatever was on the top shelf could not be seen from below. Merry stepped into the doorway of the closet and went up on her tiptoes. She reached up with both arms and felt around the top shelf with her fingers. While padding about for the camera, she was conscious of the hem of her shirt: it had risen with the upward motion of her arms. She could feel air on her exposed lower back and midriff.

"Um," Edward said, "your pants are undone."

Merry quickly lowered her arms and adjusted her shirt. "Don't look at my pants."

"I wasn't looking at your pants. Well, I was, but I wasn't looking at them on purpose."

"Well, don't look."

"I was only trying to help."

"Okay, well, thanks," Merry managed. She pretended to button her button. "What are you looking at now?"

"Sorry."

Edward dutifully turned his back and Merry went up on her tiptoes again. Her fingertips found the camera. It did look rather valuable. "Are you sure it's okay if I borrow this?"

"As long as you don't break it or lose it."

"Those aren't in my plans."

"Then why shouldn't you borrow it? It just sits there in the closet most of the time."

"You're the best."

"I think I know where there's some film," Edward said. "But put the camera in your backpack first. I didn't exactly ask if you could borrow it. They'd probably say no. Just get it back to me before the weekend."

They went downstairs to the restaurant level again. Merry followed Edward into the kitchen, where his parents, along with two members of the staff, were cooking. They all waved and smiled. Edward led Merry to a storage room in the back. He rummaged through a plastic container and found a roll of Kodak film. He handed it to Merry.

"Like I said, you're the best."

Edward opened his mouth to speak but stopped. He looked behind him. Finally, he said, "One other thing. Back there." He pointed to a set of shelves in the rear of the room. They were stacked with folded clothes wrapped in cellophane. "Those are the restaurant uniforms. The pants are pretty much the same colour as yours. All different sizes. Take one if you want. Take two if you want."

Merry ventured toward the back of the storage room. She glanced back at Edward, who turned his gaze away.

Not five minutes later, Merry was on her way out, pushing Ben Foo's front door open, when Edward's mother came running from the kitchen. "Wait!" she shouted. Merry felt sick, her face flush. Her backpack, containing a pair of uniform pants and the camera, felt suddenly heavy and conspicuous on her back. Edward's mother closed the space between kitchen door and the front door with a few, quick strides. She had something in one hand, something wrapped in a paper towel. "Your favourite," she said, smiling at Merry. "Don't leave without your favourite."

A mess of emotions coursed through her on the walk home. She hated to cry and eat, but the almond cookies were so fresh.

Merry felt like she'd not only mistreated Edward's mother, but Edward, too. She'd been angry and impatient when he was only trying to be helpful. How could he have guessed she already knew her pants were undone? How could he have ever imagined they were undone on purpose? And instead of laughing at her or, almost as bad, asking why they were undone, he simply offered her new pants. It ached to think there were people as nice as the Lams.

Nearing Lepage Street, Merry wiped her eyes with her sleeve. She pulled the camera from her backpack and, using the camera strap, let it hang around her neck. She took a bite of the last remaining cookie. When she turned the corner of Lepage, she was half a block from the blind man's house. But what she saw - who she saw - in front of it made her stop in her tracks.

Ted and two of his stoner friends were loitering out on the sidewalk, unaware of Merry's presence. They were smoking cigarettes in cupped hands, shuffling their feet, kicking at pebbles, and giggling. Merry's temples pulsed, and she felt the heat of anger on her cheeks. It ached to know there were people as rotten as Ted. She drew a deep breath and marched toward him.

Ted turned at the sound of her footsteps. He brushed cigarette ash from the front of his Guns N' Roses T-shirt. "Get out of here, Merry. Go home."

"What do you guys think you're—"

The blind man's front door opened with a squeak. All eyes turned toward it. Ted hushed his friends with a downward wave of both of his hands.

The blind man emerged from the doorway and stepped onto his little porch. With his cane before him, he descended the two steps to his front walk. His face was pointed forward, to the street, expressionless behind his dark glasses and bushy beard. He made his way down the path, his head immobile. Ted and his friends tittered and shushed each other and tittered some more. Merry shook her head in disgust and, with her thumb, checked that the film in the camera was wound.

When the blind man finally reached the edge of the sidewalk, Ted and his friends turned their backs to him. They dropped their pants and bent over, pale asses quivering with stifled laughter. Merry, on instinct, recoiled. She turned her head to one side and closed her eyes. But the weight of the camera around her neck reminded her of the opportunity and, holding the cookie between her thumb forefinger, she snapped two pictures of the scene. The sight of her brother's pimpled rear end through the viewfinder was an image, she knew, she'd not easily forget.

Then, for the first time in her life, she heard the blind man's voice. "Hello, boys." He was jovial and polite.

Ted and his friends took off running. They cackled and pulled at their pants. They hooted and slapped each other's backs and arms. When they reached the next block, Ted turned and, still jogging backwards, gave Merry the finger.

Merry stood stock still on the sidewalk, trying not to breathe. The blind man was also motionless. He cocked his head. He appeared to be listening intently. Ted and his friends were still laughing, further away now. The blind man straightened his head and sniffed the air. His nose twitched. Merry looked at the half-eaten almond cookie in her hand. She looked at the blind man. She stuffed the cookie in her pocket, feeling it crumble.

The blind man pivoted half a turn. He tucked his cane under his arm and stepped onto the grass. With his hands outstretched, he pawed the air until his palms met one of his rose bushes. Merry raised the camera to her eye. Through the viewfinder, she watched the blind man make his way slowly along the row, feeling each pink flower with a light touch. He winced from a thorn. Merry snapped a picture. The blind man stopped and turned his head. "Hello?" he ventured.

Merry took a few steps back but kept the camera to her eye. She pointed it at the front door of the house. She was startled by how badly she still wanted to see what lay beyond it. She wondered if the blind man ever felt that way, too.


Merry wore the Ben Foo pants to school the next day. They did, indeed, look much like her other pants. But these she could zip and button, and she felt a little lighter going to school without having to worry about someone seeing that her pants were undone.

Edward didn't notice, or at least pretended not to notice, that she was wearing the restaurant's pants. He shared a Thermos of pineapple chicken with her at lunch. On their way to their lockers, they crossed three older boys in the hall. After passing them, the boys turned and began to follow Merry and Edward, giggling. A feeling of dread crept all around Merry's belly. The boys pounced, and she found herself suddenly on the outside of a circle they formed around Edward. While two of them held Edward's arms, one set upon him with a roll of hockey tape. Their laughter and the squeaking of their sneakers on the polished floor of the hallway quickly attracted a crowd.

"They're taping Ben Foo's hair down!" someone zestfully announced.

Furious, Merry squeezed into the throng surrounding Edward's attackers. Finding herself directly behind one of them, she bent slightly and angled her math textbook between his legs. With her feet firmly planted, she rammed the book upward until it collided with the boy's crotch. Instantly, he doubled over and fell to the floor. Merry grabbed Edward's arm and pulled him away from the distracted mob.

"Maybe the tape would have worked," Edward said.

"Will you shut up?" Merry laughed.

On her way home from school, Merry found Ted and his friends out in front of the blind man's house again, with the blind man himself already halfway down his walk.

The boys waved their arms and crudely danced in place, unable to keep their laughter in check. Ted raised a middle finger at the blind man. One of his friends bent over, but kept his jeans on this time. Ted positioned himself behind and commenced dry humping him with, Merry noted, startling gusto. One of Ted's thrusts knocked his friend off balance, and he crumpled to the ground in laughter.

"Now, boys," the blind man said in his friendly tone, "Madame Bergeron next door tells me that you all have very attractive rear ends. However, isn't there someplace else you can go and play with each other?"

Ted and his pals took off. Merry watched them run down the street, exchanging high-fives. Like the day before, the blind man stood still and listened for a little while. Merry remained motionless on the sidewalk, keeping Edward's camera at her side. Soon, the blind man began inspecting his roses.

Merry fixed her gaze on the blue front door. How hard could it be, she posited, to stroll up the concrete path and open it? Even if the blind man heard her, she told herself, she could simply run away, unseen.

The blind man let out a loud, unabashed sneeze. Merry flinched. He thrust both hands into the pockets of his spring jacket, came away with nothing. Merry snapped a picture of him wiping his nose with his sleeve.

"Hello?"

She didn't stop running until she reached her own driveway.


Her mother was waiting for her when she walked in the door. Before Merry even had time to remove her backpack, her mother extended one arm out straight, the pants Merry had worn the day before dangling from her hand. She reached into one of the pockets with her other hand and came away with a handful of almond cookie crumbs. "I thought I instructed you to stop eating at that place."

"Mom!"

"Don't *Mom* me! You have defied me for - wait. What are you wearing?"

"Clothes."

"Merry, seriously. Whose pants are those?"

"Mine, obviously."

"They are *not*. Come closer."

"Aw, Mom!" Merry turned toward the hallway, hoping to escape to her room.

"Stop right there!" Her mother strode toward her. "Where did you get those pants?"

"It doesn't matter."

An expression of horror came over her mother's face. "Did you steal them from somewhere? Merry, don't tell me you stole them!"

"Mom. Come on."

"Where did you get them?"

"They're from the restaurant," Merry said quietly, looking down at her feet.

"From the restaurant? The restaurant? You're *working* there now? That's *child labour!*"

"Mom! I am not working there!"

"Then what are you doing with those pants?"

"Edward *gave* them to me."

"Why in the world would Edward give you a pair of pants?"

"Because he's kind, Mom." Merry slipped her backpack off and unzipped it. She removed the camera. "He's actually nice and kind. Could you imagine that?"

She stormed from the house.


Merry's angry march brings her back to the blind man's street. He is still out in his front yard, now tending to the other row of rose bushes. Again, Merry eyes the front door. She holds her breath and creeps to the edge of the sidewalk where the blind man's front walk begins. She glances at him, letting her breath out slowly; he is ever busy with his flowers.

*Wouldn't it be something*, she thinks, *to know what it looks like inside, to be the only one who knows?* To see what her mother has always wanted to gawk at, and to never tell her a thing about it? The knowledge would be Merry's alone, leaving her mother to go on with her little curiosities, to go on with her idiotic concerns about MSG and suburban child labour.

Merry tiptoes up the walk and lightly mounts the two steps to the small porch. With her heart knocking inside her chest, she turns to look at the blind man. His back is to her, oblivious to her presence. Just one picture, she tells herself. Two at the most. She faces the blue front door and grips the door handle with her fingers, resting her thumb upon the latch. The brass feels cold and unfamiliar. Merry breathes deeply and presses with her thumb as gently as she can manage, trying to keep the latch from making a sound. She pushes the door open a few inches and, before she has time to change her mind, slips inside the blind man's house.

She finds herself inside a small vestibule. There is a sliding closet door on one side and, installed on the opposite wall, a coat rack. An oval mirror hangs above the coat rack. Merry smiles at the light coating of dust covering its glass surface. She looks at her reflection in the mirror and raises Edward's camera to the level of her neck. She takes a picture of herself, taking a picture.

Tentatively, she ventures from the vestibule and enters a short hallway. It goes in three directions: left, right, and straight ahead. Before her is the kitchen. To the left, a longer hallway with three doors. To her right is the living room, where two couches face each other, a coffee table of dark wood between them. Merry turns right.

The coffee table holds a spiny aloe vera plant in a green plastic pot, an empty teacup in a saucer, and a small white plate, bare but for a few toast crumbs and a sprig of lettuce. There are more potted plants – ferns – on other surfaces in the room. And, in a corner next to the window, on top of a melamine table, sits a television set.

*You owe me a million bucks, Mom,* Merry thinks.

There is a stone fireplace installed in the far wall. A painting hangs above the mantelpiece. Merry creeps over for a closer look. Unmistakeably, the subject of the painting is the blind man's house: she notes the white siding, the blue door and shutters, the concrete walk, and the rose bushes in full, pink bloom. A line of chill creeps across Merry's shoulders as she observes a figure standing in the yard in the painting: the blind man himself, with his cane, his glasses, his beard. She snaps a picture of the painting.

She feels fright weighing down – she's been inside the house for too long. She starts toward the vestibule but the squeak of the front door makes her stop beside the coffee table. Merry's stomach cramps. Seeking a place to hide, she takes a step to her left, then to her right. She takes a step backwards, bumping her calf against the corner of the coffee table with a thump. The teacup clinks in the saucer. Merry raises her leg as if to take the move back. Her balance shifts and she pivots on one foot, causing her balance to deteriorate. She aims her fall at the nearest couch and flops into it in a sitting position.

"Hello?" The blind man appears in the little hallway. "Is someone there?"

Facing him from the couch, Merry doesn't move. She hardly breathes. The blind man stands completely still. He looks like he might in a photograph: frozen.

Finally, the blind man stirs. He tucks his cane under his arm and enters the living room. He moves slowly, but with noticeable assuredness. Merry is nearly certain that he can see her. But though he walks in her general direction, his face is pointed away from her, toward the corner of the room where the television is. Though terrified, Merry forces herself to raise the camera to her eye. Through the viewfinder, the blind man looks very much like he has looked to her all her life: the big sunglasses, the bushy beard, the vaguely dishevelled clothes, and the slanted angle with which he holds his head. Up close, though, there is one other thing: Merry detects expression in the blind man's face. Despite the dark glasses and the obscuring beard, it is so clear. The blind man is afraid.

Her mother's obsession with this man is pathetic. Her brother's disrespect for him is disgraceful. But what word, Merry wonders, to describe her own use of him? Are her actions any nobler than those of a busybody and a scumbag? Merry lowers the camera from her eye.

She snaps open the camera's back compartment, exposing the film to the extinguishing light. A new idea for a photography project is already forming in her mind. She tugs at the film with her fingers. It unspools like ribbon.

Again, the blind man cries, "Hello?"

Merry rises from the couch. "Hi."

# SOMETHING IMPORTANT
# AND DELICATE

Every year in the last week of summer, just before school started, the carnival came to town. It took up most of the parking lot of the strip mall on top of the hill, overlooking the autoroute. The Carousel, Tea Cups, The Matterhorn, and Moby Dick materialized like visiting relatives from far away, mysterious yet familiar, in town for a few days, looking slightly older than they did the year before.

Dad was the biggest carnival fan. He talked it up throughout the summer, the anticipation mushrooming by August. "Carnival's coming!"

They arrived in a caravan of trucks, trailers, and campers. Sinewy, weather-worn women and men, Styrofoam coffee cups and king-size cigarettes. It took them three days to set everything up. Dad took Lawrence and me on walks down to the strip mall to check on their progress. He made us pancakes for dinner on opening night. He went with us on all the rides he wasn't too tall for, and for the real kiddie rides he rooted us on with hollers and whoops from just the other side of the barriers. He was crazy for The Cobra, a mini coaster that we always saved for the end of the night. He wished he could have ridden it with us; I thought he would crawl right through the metal bars of the barrier sometimes he was so excited.

Dad collected his empties all year long, stockpiling them in one end of the garage. Winter nights as a kid, I'd trot happily from the living room to the fridge and back again, cradling beer after beer for him, one hand around the cold neck of the bottle, the other supporting the base. "That's a pal." I just wanted those bottles emptied. I never could convince Mom to take one, though. She said the same thing about beer that she said about the carnival. "I'm not crazy about it."

In August, Dad would transfer his hoard of bottles from the garage to the back of the station wagon and, in two trips, return them to the dépanneur at the strip mall. For the occasion, Roland Quinn, who owned and operated the store, allowed us to drive around to the back, where he'd unlatch his delivery door. Dad, Lawrence, and I made a chain from the car to the door, passing all those six-packs, twelves, and two-fours of empties into Quinn's place. With the money Dad got he bought us our carnival tickets, unlimited passes, all four nights, with pocket change for Whack-A-Mole and Skee-Ball.

The year I started Grade Eleven, the carnival came late. It was the end of September and it had turned cold, drizzling on and off. We still went but Lawrence had wandered out to Banff after spending the summer cleaning oil barrels in the Arctic and I was looking forward more to hanging out with Angie Hart than with Dad. By then Brad, or *the vasectomy malfunction*, as I overheard my mother call him one night through the closed door of my parents' bedroom, was eight. It bugged the hell out of Dad that he'd never had the guts to get on The Cobra. "Your brothers rode it when they were four!" That year Brad announced he was finally ready. It was cruel, but I told him it was probably too late, that he was too tall now. Brad started to snivel. Dad coached him to slouch.

When we got to the carnival, I spotted Angie and her friends near the snack bar. After Dad gave me my bracelet pass, I told him I'd catch up with him and Brad later. Dad glanced over at the gang of girls. They wore tight jeans and puffy coats. Long wool scarves dangled from around their necks. They laughed and whispered, clutching plastic cups, sipping through straws. Dad patted me on the back, his eyes proud, like I was a soldier or a quarterback. It made me cringe.

"Okay, pal. Just be sure to find us in time to see Brad on the Cobra. It's important his big brother be there." His breath was foul. He'd already started in on next year's bottle collection.

I sauntered over to the girls and made like I was interested in the snack bar menu. I said hey to Angie.

"Hey, too."

I asked her if she had started thinking about that English assignment. She said she was doing it on *The Shining* because she'd read it over the summer and was planning to coast as much as possible this year. I said I wasn't sure what I was going to do but a Stephen King book seemed like a cool idea. Her friends giggled and whispered, shared knowing looks. Vicky Dufour was the least subtle of them. "Well, we'll just leave you two alone." Her friends slunk away. Angie made a show of protest but she didn't leave with them.

Every part of me was electric.

Angie had the darkest black hair, down just past her shoulders. Baby-blue ski jacket and a white scarf. She wore braces, new from the summer, and I'd noticed at school how she concealed her mouth with the back of her hand now when she smiled or laughed. Angie's eyes were small, brown, and intense. Her left earlobe held twin green studs. The second piercing was also new from the summer. I wondered if she'd had permission to do that or if she'd just done it.

Once Angie's friends were out of sight, we both got quiet. She looked at the ground and twirled the end of her scarf around her hand. Undid it and twirled it again. "It's cold, eh?"

"Yeah."

I invited Angie on The Spook Train. She didn't have a bracelet or any tickets but I had a pocketful of loonies and paid for her. We got the back car of the train and it wasn't too packed, either.

When I was a kid, I always sat beside Dad on The Spook Train. Lawrence had to sit in the car behind or in front of us, alone, or sometimes with another kid from another odd-numbered group. Dad called him a big guy for doing it. The Spook Train entered The Haunted Tunnel through an arched cut-out in the ride's façade just big enough for us to pass under. Inside it was dark like night. And all around us in the blackness were shiny animal eyes; red, yellow, and white, with a litany of howls, hoots, and growls sounding in the background. After the train turned a rough corner, a green spotlight would snap on to the left of us, revealing a skeleton dressed in a train engineer's overalls and cap, slumped against a rock. All of the sudden the skeleton's teeth would start to chatter to the tune of insane, tormented laughter. Dad would laugh, too, and softly squeeze my shoulder. He knew I was scared but he didn't let anyone else know it. He just went on laughing, pretending we were all having the same good time, keeping a hand on my shoulder when Frankenstein's monster popped out at us, when the wolves snarled, when the ghosts rattled their chains.

The Spook Train car was small enough that my arm and Angie's couldn't help but rest against each other, jacket to jacket. I ventured a bit, cautiously, with my hand and brushed hers with the back of mine, making like it was incidental, and left it there, a minor meeting of flesh. She didn't move, didn't flinch. The train started with a jerk and as soon as we were in the dark of the tunnel, I sensed her pivot in her seat. I turned, too, and our mouths came together. Angie's tongue tasted faintly of Coke.

We were still kissing when the train exited the tunnel. Angie pulled away abruptly. We were back out in the cold air, the commotion of the carnival. Angie looked down at her lap and played with the end of her scarf again. We got out of the car and followed the other riders out through the opening in the barrier. We were quiet again. We lingered in front of The Spook Train, the carnival crowds flowing around us. I asked her if she wanted to ride again. She said no. I felt a hollow open up inside of me. But then she took my hand and started walking, pulled me with her. "Let's go watch the autoroute."

We walked through the games alley. An operator with bad teeth implored me to play Balloon Darts. "*Tu peux gagner un prix pour ta blonde!*" I squeezed Angie's hand and she squeezed back. I looked at her, caught her eye. For a second, she smiled at me, shyly, then looked down. She picked up the pace, started jogging, and tugged me out of the alley. We were right in front of The Cobra.

I could see Dad and Brad in line. Dad kept looking back and forth between his beloved coaster and the surrounding crowds. He was on the lookout for me. It wasn't so bad that he made Brad do everything Lawrence and I had done, I just didn't see why I had to relive it all, too. It wasn't my fault Brad didn't have a brother his own size.

"Isn't that your little bro?"

"Yeah."

"He's cute. He looks like you. Want to go say hi?"

"Nah." I motioned toward The Matterhorn, the hill behind it, the autoroute. Angie hesitated but followed.

We sat on the grass on the slope of the hill, maybe halfway down to the pavement of the autoroute. There were four Grade Nines a little further over, a little further down, boys, sharing a green shaker of Kraft Parmesan, licking their palms. It was windier on the hill than in the thick of the carnival. Angie wrapped her arms around one of my arms and leaned on my shoulder. The moon was more than half-full with a bright halo glow all around it. Cars and trucks whipped by in both directions beneath us, headlights bright like the animal eyes on The Spook Train.

"My dad drives a rig," Angie said.

"I know."

"He's home Sundays and Mondays."

"Is that a good thing or a bad thing?"

"I don't know. It's always been like that."

I slipped my arm from Angie's grip and put it around her shoulder.

"When I was a little kid, I thought my dad was driving every truck I saw," Angie continued, staring at the autoroute. "I remember once, my mom was driving me to skating and there was this rig up ahead of us and I got all excited because I was sure it was him. My mom laughed and said he was halfway to Chicoutimi. I insisted it was him. She just laughed some more. I was so mad at her. She wouldn't even speed up to check. To prove it wasn't him. I was just supposed to believe her."

"You took skating lessons?"

"Who didn't?"

"Me."

"Well, who didn't that's a girl?"

We watched the cars and trucks some more.

I moved my head toward Angie's, sought out her lips. She kept looking at the autoroute and I had to probe around with my face. She kissed me back but she didn't open her mouth like on The Spook Train. In the middle of it she pulled back, looked down at the grass. I bobbed for another kiss.

"I'm cold."

"It was your idea to come down here," I snapped. I felt Angie withdraw. She turned her head away. My words replayed in my head, nastier with each echo. It felt like I'd broken something, something important and delicate. "Sorry," I started.

A ray of bright white light, right in my face.

"You two! You can't be here!" Ken, the mall cop. We called him that but really, he was just the janitor. He hated kids.

"I was just leaving." Angie sprang to her feet and marched swiftly up the hill with arms crossed. I watched her go, watched her disappear at the top while Ken scattered the cheese kids with threats to call their fathers.

"Tough luck, kid," Ken said to me, shaking his head. He reached into the inside pocket of his jacket and pulled out a pack of Export A green. "Now get!"

I heard a scream from above. The carnival was full of screams but this one was different. Instead of fun scared it was just scared. There was a rumbling of voices, mounting alarm, an uproar. Ken stuffed his cigarettes back into his pocket and ran up the hill. I followed.

A hundred people at least were clustered around The Cobra and more were on the way, running from different parts of the carnival, all of them curious, nosy, morbid. I was gripped by a sudden, abysmal queasiness. I pushed into the thick crowd, slipping between gawkers up on their tiptoes, necks craned, chattering, giggling. I could see the coaster parked in its start position, a collection of little kids aboard with the safety bars down, waiting, fidgeting, horsing around. Brad's face was fire-engine red. He was in the last car, sobbing. A girl of four, maybe five, was sitting next to him, both arms raised high in the air, screaming delight, even though the ride wasn't even moving. I got frantic, fought my way deeper into the crowd. I wondered where the ride operator could possibly be. That nobody had attended to Brad yet, to whatever was wrong with him, filled me with fear and outrage.

"Don't worry, son," a man's voice said near my ear. "We'll get him out. We'll get him out fast." It was Roland Quinn. He was forcing his way through the crowd, too, one arm straight out in front of him, the other held straight up in the air. "*Tassez-vous!* Make way!" Above the throng, in Quinn's hand, a jar of Vaseline.

Quinn grabbed my arm and together we ploughed the rest of the way through. We made it to the barrier and Quinn unlatched the unattended metal gate himself. I started toward Brad but Quinn directed me off to the side instead. People were pressed up all along the barrier, mall cop Ken and a couple of carnival workers urging them back. Dad was right at the front of one section of the crowd, hunched over but looking up. He saw me coming and gave me a big thumbs-up. I couldn't figure out which side of the barrier he was on.

Because he was on both.

Somehow, Dad had squeezed his head through two of the bars and now, clearly, he was wedged there. Apparently, every inch had counted on Brad's big night. "Hey, pal!" Dad called to me, enthusiastically, like we had just run into each other by chance at a hot dog stand.

Mr. Quinn approached Dad and put a hand on top of his head, gently guided him to bend it down, the way a barber would. He applied a glob of Vaseline to the back and sides of Dad's neck. "We'll get you out, Dan," Quinn chuckled. "Don't you worry. We'll try and slip you out with this. Fire department's on the way with cutters. One way or the other, we'll get you out."

I stepped up. Embarrassed and determined at the same time.

"Can I help?"

"Your brother, pal."

I sprang off, jogged to the base of the coaster's platform and flew up the stairs. Brad's grubby cheeks were streaked with tears but he wasn't crying anymore. He was smiling, laughing even. Angie was there, crouched beside him, chatting away, a hand on the back of his head, stroking his hair, looking important and delicate.

# BODY NOISES WITH
# THE DOOR OPEN

She was mad at him for smoking on their vacation. He said, "Come on, it's a vacation," and tipped his ash into one of his empties.

On the way to breakfast she caught him eyeballing one of the other hotel guests, a woman wearing brown capris and a cream tank top. Tan freckled chest. "Can you be a little more obvious?"

They spent the rest of the day by the lake, sitting on wooden deck chairs. She had a stack of *Better Homes & Gardens*. He watched her read for a while. He felt like smoking but not the disapproval. He fell asleep. When he woke up his forehead stung.

It felt crispy when he blinked or moved his eyebrows.

That night he was in the bathroom with the door open, shaving off the prickly vacation beard that was wrecking all of his chances for sex. She was on the couch, watching a repeat of *Friends* they'd seen together in the Nineties.

His chin and cheeks smooth and clean, a third of the way through his moustache, he put the razor down on the counter. He watched his own face in the mirror as the gas built up in the base of his throat, until it couldn't be contained. He let the burp out; let it out as loud as it wanted. The laugh track on the TV started up a second later, the timing impeccable, and it made him laugh, too. He opened his throat and allowed more gas to surface. Forced out a second burp, this time uttering some passable facsimile of the word "burp" with the burp. The TV failed to comply this time and his thoughts turned to finding an excuse to go get something, anything, in the car so he could smoke on the way to it and on the way back. He sniffed, snorted, horked, and spat in the sink. He belched again without really noticing it.

TV muted and she went after him from the couch. Said she was disappointed in him. That he only thought of himself, making body noises with the door open. The people in the next room were out on their patio – she said she could see the candlelight glow – and with the patio door open they'd probably heard him.

He felt sorry for himself, having wasted a perfectly good vacation beard.

# SPRING TRAINING

My grandfather went down to West Palm Beach every March. For two weeks he left the cold and the wet to my grandmother and me. Neither of us sat in his La-Z-Boy while he was away but we watched all the game shows and *Alice* reruns we wanted.

Every year during those two weeks my grandmother would paint the whole house. I'd just get used to eating in a blue kitchen and then it would be yellow. Once, she painted the living room pink. When my sunburned grandfather got home, he squinted, shook his head, said "Jeez," and sat down in his chair and put on the hockey game.

The year I was six we had a very warm March. My grandmother taught me the word *unseasonably*. The kitchen was green.

"Why don't we go to spring training?" I asked over grilled cheese and chocolate milk.

"It's not for ladies and little boys."

"Why not?"

My grandmother lit a cigarette and put away the milk. She ran water in the sink.

"This sandwich is unseasonably good."

Smoky kiss on the back of my neck.

The year the kitchen was brown my grandmother played a trick on my grandfather. She lay down in bed, covers up to her chin, and said, "Go watch for him in the window. When he gets home, tell him Nanny's tired."

"Tired?"

"Tell him Nanny's been asleep since Tuesday."

"But—"

"It's just a joke. Go watch for him."

When my grandfather arrived, a man got out of the car with him. They came up the walk together, both of their faces red like lobsters. I didn't know the man. He was tall and had a big stomach and wore a yellow turtleneck tucked into a pair of plaid pants. He had enormous sunglasses that covered not only his eyes but almost his whole nose, too.

I went out on the balcony. "Nanny went to bed on Tuesday."

"Eh?"

"Nanny went to bed on Tuesday and she's still asleep."

"Jeez."

My grandfather mounted the stairs and brushed past me into the house.

The man came up on the balcony. He breathed hard. "Look at this, kid." He handed me a pen. There was a small picture on it, a lady wearing a black dress. "Now hold it up straight." I tipped the pen upright. The picture began to change. The man chuckled. Slowly, the lady's dress disappeared and soon she was naked.

My grandmother came outside. She was holding her arm and she looked tired for real. I closed my fingers around the pen but part of it stuck out and she grabbed my wrist and I opened my hand again.

"What do you think you're doing? He's just a little boy."

"Sorry, lady. Just a joke."

The day got more fun after that. My grandmother and I walked up to Quinn's and she bought me a pepperoni stick and a Kit Kat. We walked all over and didn't even go home until dark.

# PSYCHIC RADIO

Friday night was a lonely place.

The house felt segmented: Alex's father was installed in the living room with the television and VCR under his control, watching the shows he'd filled his personal video tape with throughout the week; his mother was in the kitchen, amid her bowls, tins, measuring cups, and bags of Quaker brand mixes, baking muffins, cookies, and other snacks that she'd dole out sparingly (she had hiding places all over the house) over the coming days; and Alex's younger brother, John, was in his own room, as usual, playing.

Alex listened from the other side of John's closed bedroom door. At the age of thirteen, just three years younger than Alex, John still played with Transformers, He-Man, and Star Wars action figures. His bed was a menagerie of stuffed animals, accumulated since he was a baby: bears, dogs, cats, two owls, a seal, a tiger, a Cookie Monster, and a Bert.

It was revolting.

John's favourite stuffed animal was a grey dog with floppy brown ears named Droopy One. With stained and threadbare fur, one arm hanging by a few threads and one ear kept in place now with staples, Droopy One was by far the oldest in John's collection. Alex had, in fact, been the stuffed dog's original owner, from a time before John was born, from a time when its name had been, simply, Droopy.

At around the age of two, John had begun to fixate on Droopy. He cried whenever he saw Alex holding it, he stole it from Alex's bed whenever the opportunity arose. Either transgression made Alex feel entitled to cuff or strangle his little brother, and he exercised his perceived rights somewhat ruthlessly. Their mother tried to bring peace to the house by introducing a new stuffed animal to the mix, another dog, telling John, "This is Droopy, too." John happily adopted the newcomer, calling it Droopy Two (what he believed he'd heard its name to be), but never stopped coveting Alex's dog, which he began referring to as Droopy One.

The battle had continued for another two years until Alex, feigning the indifference he thought he was supposed to feel as a seven-year-old boy, finally gave up Droopy for good.

Through John's door, Alex could hear incessant dialogue. John played with his toys, the stuffed animals included, in combination, providing a voice for every inanimate object in his collection. There were macho voices and girly ones, British accents and southern drawls. Animal speech was interspersed with growls, barks, hoots, and meows.

Alex could only listen to that for so long.

He turned from John's door, traipsed down the hallway, and slipped into his bedroom, his own Friday night section of the house.

His bed was unmade, two of the four drawers of his dresser were half open, and the floor was littered with clothes and schoolbooks. Along the wall beside his door, however, was a small sanctum of order: Alex's stereo and his record collection; the record jackets sat neatly in two orange milk crates on the floor, and, except for when he was changing a record, the lid over the turntable always remained closed.

Delicately, Alex dropped the needle on his copy of *Fresh Fruit for Rotting Vegetables*. He pushed the volume dial up past seven, bordering on eight. Finding the highest possible volume setting on his record player without drawing the attention of either one of his parents was an ongoing experiment. He took the album jacket in hand and crawled onto his bed, on top of his unmade sheets. He lay back and for the umpteenth time studied the cover art: a grainy, black and white photograph of a line of police cars engulfed in flames.

He heard stomping from outside his closed bedroom door, drawing nearer, and he was in no way surprised.

The imminent visit was, he knew, completely avoidable. But the Dead Kennedys sounded so much better played loud.

The door opened, just wide enough for his mother to poke her head inside. "Could we please turn the head-banging down a little?"

Her attempt to be hip, her use of jargon gleamed from some *20/20* piece or *People* magazine article about punk rock, gave Alex the same sick, embarrassed feeling he had when he walked too close to his mother at the mall. He could not bring himself to acknowledge her words. Instead, he cupped his left ear and turned it toward the doorway. "I can't hear you," he lied.

His mother pushed the door open all the way and barged into the room, making for the record player. Alex sprang from his bed but it was already too late. Jello Biafra's warbling lisp was abruptly cut off by a terrible, grating scratch of needle on vinyl.

"Oh, thanks a lot," Alex wailed. "It's probably ruined. Thanks a whole lot."

"You should have put it lower when I asked you."

"I couldn't *hear* you."

"Then you only have yourself to blame."

Alex took a step toward his record player. His mother blocked him. "That's enough for tonight. Why don't you do something else?"

"Like go to the party at Simon Lundquist's? Oh, I guess not *that*, since I'm *not allowed*."

"So you can drink yourself sick like the others and come home in an ambulance?"

"Ambulances don't bring you home," Alex scoffed. "They bring you to the hospital."

"Exactly."

Alex slapped the sides of his thighs with the palms of both hands. "Mom, *everybody's* going to the party."

"As far as I'm concerned, this discussion is over. It ended two hours ago."

From the kitchen, the oven's exhausted timer sounded its feeble chime. Alex's mother turned on her heel to attend to it.

Alex closed his door, then pivoted and leaned his back against it. Slowly, he sank down until he was sitting on the floor. He drew his arms around his knees and thought how unfair it was, to be locked up like a prisoner every weekend while kids from school went to parties.

He wondered if he'd feel better or worse about it if he actually got invited to parties.


Sitting on the floor with his back against his door for the rest of the night had, at first, seemed like a good idea. However, after realizing no one could actually see (and therefore pity) him, Alex quickly grew bored of it. He crawled to his stereo and positioned himself on the floor in front of it. He slid the volume button down to four and pressed the RADIO button.

Static spat from the speakers. Alex fiddled with the tuning dial. He came upon a Paul Anka song and quickly moved on. He found the baseball game. He turned the dial some more. He came upon a commercial for a car dealership. He kept going. He found the baseball game in French. He switched to the FM band.

A woman, her voice soft and gentle, was speaking. "I've got this incredible tingly feeling. All over." Quiet wind chimes rang sporadically in the background. "I'm here, sitting in this chair, in this studio. This I know. But I also know that my voice is out *there*, dancing on your radio waves. And that – just imagining that – makes me tingle."

The woman sighed. "It's as if the entire cosmos, with millions of tiny, kind and gentle hands, is tickling me." Her delivery was slow and dreamy. She giggled in a way that made Alex wonder if she was on drugs. "Welcome, people. Welcome all you beautiful people out there. Welcome to *Psychic Radio.*"

Alex pictured the woman behind the voice in a darkened radio studio, surrounded by lit candles and piles of loose flowers, a thin column of incense smoke curling up to the ceiling. He imagined her as a never-reformed hippie, with long and curly hair, and a thin band tied around her forehead. He saw her wearing a tasselled buckskin vest over a sarong. She sounded, he thought, like the type of person who owned her own gong.

And while Alex would have been too embarrassed to use the radio host's word *tingly* to describe what he was feeling, he was conscious that a sort of spark had been lit inside of him. His awareness was heightened, and his head swam somewhat. His shoulders and the back of his neck felt cool. This show, whatever it was, wherever it was coming from, was exactly the kind of weirdness that, Alex had recently come to understand, he was voracious for. He scooted closer to one of his speakers and leaned in.

The host's name was Mitra. She gave out a phone number and invited listeners to call in for their choice of a psychic reading or a past-life reading. She asked someone named Elliott if there were any callers waiting. Elliott, in a voice even softer than Mitra's, chimed in to say there were no callers yet, but he predicted there would be some soon. This was followed by a few seconds of dead air. Then Mitra's voice returned. "Was that a joke, Elliott?" she asked eagerly. "Because you said you *predicted* there would be callers. Was that a joke? A psychic joke?" Elliott confirmed his line had, in fact, been a joke. Mitra's laughter boomed from Alex's speakers. Elliott tittered in the background. Alex couldn't help but laugh a little, too.

Soon, someone did call; a woman named Angel. Mitra offered some friendly and enthusiastic hellos. She complimented Angel on her name. She asked Angel what she was calling in for.

"I'm looking to get a past-life reading. Please."

"Okay," Mitra sang. "Okay. What I'm going to need you to do is say your name, and then tell me your date of birth."

"Um, alright," Angel replied, giggling a little. "Um. I'm Angel. I was born on April 2, 1961."

"Okay, Angel," Mitra hummed. "Okay, let's see. Okay. Oh. Okay. Let's see. Okay, alright." The stereo speakers grew quiet and Alex held his breath to hear. For some moments, Mitra's own breathing, and a few short, contemplative moans were all that came over the air. "Oh," she said suddenly. "This is interesting."

Mitra informed Angel that in her life prior to the one she was living now, she had been a Japanese man, born in or around 1920. And, during the Second World War, her previous self had been a soldier. A good soldier, who always followed orders, and who was proud to fight for the Empire. His platoon had been stationed on an island in the Pacific and, soon after, came under heavy shelling from an American warship. "You operated a rocket launcher," Mytra said, "but you hardly managed to fire it. Bombs were falling all around you, and early on in the battle, an explosion knocked you unconscious. When you woke up, you found that you were, except for a few dozen scattered dead bodies, completely alone."

"Wow," Angel said.

"And it didn't end there," Mitra replied. "For days, you searched all over the island. You found that you were, indeed, alone. You were extremely disappointed. You understood that your outfit had most likely been overwhelmed by the attack and had abandoned the island, leaving you behind in the confusion. But you didn't blame anyone but yourself. You felt like you had failed in your duties, and you were itching to rejoin the fight. So you did all you could to stay alive and ready, ready for the day when you would be rescued from the island and put back into the war. And that's what you did, Angel. That's what you did for nearly ten years!"

"Oh!"

"Within just a few months of being marooned on that island, the war ended. But you had no idea! You didn't have a clue! In your mind, the war was still going on, and you went about your business on the island, staying ready, surviving in order to fight again someday. Imagine that, never knowing the war was over!"

Alex laughed out loud. Part of him was genuinely enthralled; the part of him that liked to believe in things like Bigfoot and UFOs. Another part of him was skeptical; the part of him that was well-versed in *Gilligan's Island* lore. He couldn't help but think of an episode he'd seen a few times over the years in which a Japanese soldier, unaware World War II is over, arrives on the island in a submarine and proceeds to capture and imprison the American castaways.

Either way, Alex was thoroughly impressed. If Mitra really could read people's past-lives, then she was a powerful physic. But even if she was making it all up, taking advantage of gullible listeners, she was still a tremendous storyteller.

Whatever the truth was, it was the greatest thing Alex had ever heard on the radio.

As he continued to listen, he began to notice a recurrent sound: a clinking that, at first, he thought were Mitra's wind chimes. But there was something strangely familiar about the rhythm and, focusing on it, Alex realized it was not coming from the radio at all. The clinking was happening outside his bedroom door.

From his spot on the floor in front of the stereo, Alex crawled quietly to the door. The clinking continued from the other side and, in the crack between the floor and the bottom edge of the door, Alex could see two feet in a pair of white socks. Swiftly, abruptly, he sprang from the floor and yanked open his door.

It was John. Standing in the hallway, facing Alex, stirring a cup of tea. His eyebrows rose slightly, expectantly.

"What do you think *you're* doing?" Alex spat.

"I was wondering what you were laughing about." John's real voice was high-pitched; another source of irritation for Alex.

He nearly slammed the door in John's face but he heard Elliott tell Mitra she had another caller. Alex turned in the radio's direction. Then he turned back to John. He bit his bottom lip and stood aside in the doorway, signalling his brother inside with a nod of the head. John glowed with happiness. Alex rolled his eyes.

The new caller asked for a reading. John looked at Alex quizzically but Alex shushed him before he could utter a word. Mitra asked the caller to state his name and birthdate. "Simon," came the reply. "November 15, 1950."

Again, John looked at Alex with a confused expression. "She's a *psychic*," Alex snapped. John's eyes widened and his mouth formed the shape of an O. He edged a little closer to the speakers.

Like with the previous caller, silence prevailed for a time. Alex glanced at John. His younger brother had a very particular way of drinking tea. He never placed his cup to his lips. Instead, he spooned each sip, slurping quietly. Alex looked away.

"I think, Simon," Mitra began, "that you sometimes, maybe not so much hide, but don't *display* the skills that you have. You don't show them off as much as you might really like to. You feel blocked. That's why you maybe don't apply yourself as much as you know you're capable of applying yourself."

"Oh, wow," said Simon, sounding dumfounded.

"And you've got to remember," Mitra went on, "that you are an inventor: the inventor of your own destiny."

Alex thought he could hear the caller gasp into his telephone. "That's amazing," Simon said. "You hit it right on the head. Thank you. You're right. You are so right. Thank you so much."

"Whoa," John said.

"Lucky guess," Alex scoffed, trying to act cool.

John looked at him like he was insane.

They listened to more callers. There were additional past-life readings – a nineteenth-century woman from North Carolina who posed as a man all of her adult life, ran her own farm, and for a few years drove a section of the Underground Railroad; a convict from the slums of London who wound up in an Australian penal colony in the late 1700s and served as a healer for his fellow inmates; a Chinese explorer who walked all the way to the Persian Gulf in the 1500s only to die from choking on a chicken bone. There were other psychic readings, as well as general information and advice about jobs, love, and happiness.

After half an hour of listening, John took his teacup and left Alex's room. "Where are you going?" Alex asked. He was surprised to feel genuinely disappointed. He stayed by the radio, assuming, actually hoping, John would come back.

Some minutes later Alex heard John's soft, high-pitched voice on the radio, giving his name and birthdate to Mitra.

"1974?" Mitra practically squealed. "So that makes you, let's see—"

"I'm thirteen."

"A first-year teenager! Wow, how fun! Thank you for calling, John. What can I do for you?"

"Um, I'd like to get a reading?"

Alex poked his head out into the hallway. A telephone cord ran from his parents' bedroom to John's closed door, where it passed beneath it. Alex darted back inside his room, to his stereo speakers.

"Okay, John," Mitra said, "let's see what we see here. Hmmm. Okay, so John: you're thirteen."

"Uh, yes."

"Okay, I'm trying. Okay. Hmmm. Oh! I'm seeing something: animals. I'm seeing a lot of animals. Do you live on a farm, John?"

"Um, no."

Mitra exhaled audibly. "Wow. It's really strong, the animal image. I'm seeing animals."

"I have a cat," John offered.

"It's much more than that," Mitra giggled. "I'm seeing several animals. Rows of them, maybe. Do you live near a farm, or do you have relatives with a farm that you might visit?"

"Um, no. But I do like animals."

"*That's* really clear," Mitra laughed. "But there's more. There's a real presence. Of animals." But for Mitra's sighs, the radio went quiet for a nearly a full minute. Finally, she said, "Okay, well that's just really strange. I can't put my finger on this animal thing. But anyway—"

"Um, I have a lot of stuffed animals."

"What's that?"

"I said I have a lot of stuffed animals."

The radio went completely silent. Then Mitra released a long, loud sound that was one part sigh and one part moan, a mixture of relief and ecstasy. A prickling sensation seized the skin on the back of Alex's neck. "Oh!" Mitra cried. "Oh! Teddy bears!" She laughed happily, enthusiastically. Elliott could be heard laughing in the background, too. Alex, despite himself, smiled and sighed. "The animals I was seeing," Mitra began again, "they were so alive. It was so confusing. But now I see it. I understand. The animals were alive to me because they're alive to you! Aren't they, John?"

After a pause, John answered, "Yes."

"Wow," Mitra said. "John, just wow. Phew...that felt good. That felt really good. John, listen to me: you call back anytime, okay?"

"Um, okay."

Alex left his room and jogged down the hall. He opened John's door. His brother was sitting on the bed, a look of awe etched on his face. He was cradling the telephone receiver to his chest. His stuffed animals, Droopy One and all, encircled him.


John's most prized possession was his BMX. It was silver, with a blue seat and matching blue handle grips. It was a present for his thirteenth birthday from his grandparents. He'd wanted a new bicycle but he never expected to get a BMX. He wasn't even sure if his grandparents knew the difference between a BMX and a regular bike. When his grandfather pulled it out from the trunk of his car, saying *Surprise*, John jumped up and down. It was the greatest bike he had ever seen. Alex, who'd been leaning against the garage door, kicked a rock across the driveway and, walking away, said, "What are *you* going to do with a BMX?"

There were kids at school who knew how to do tricks on their BMXs. The only trick John knew, and it was one the other BMXers would not have considered a real trick, was to ride to the top of the grassy hill behind his old elementary school. The hill was not particularly high – it stood about as tall as three cars stacked on top of one another – but it was steep. John had to acquire some speed and momentum before attempting the climb.

The morning after talking to Mitra on the radio, John was riding his bike, alone, behind the school. Heading along the concrete path toward the hill, John stood up to pedal faster. He passed the monkey bars. He sped past the slide, the swings, and the garbage can. His front tire hit the base of the hill and John's body bent backward; he was pedalling forward but his eyes were on the sky. He felt horizontal. Seconds later, he was vertical again, sitting on his seat atop the hill. Breathing heavily, he patted the bar between his bike's handle grips. "Good one, Maximilian," he said, using the name he'd given to his BMX.

John got off his bike and laid it down gently on the grass. He lay down beside it, and stared at the cloudless blue sky. Alex had been just as amazed as John had been, at least at first. Alex said it was freaky, totally freaky, that Mitra could see John's animals. After the call, the two rehashed it for nearly an hour in Alex's room. Alex played his records all the while, changing them after a song or two, mentioning the names of the bands as he did, and offered the album covers to John to look at. Alex played The Smiths, Butthole Surfers, Camper Van Beethoven, Bow Wow Wow, and Wall of Voodoo. John had heard them all before, but pretended it was all new to him; it had been a long time since he and Alex had done something together, and John could never let his older brother know he regularly snuck into his room to listen to his music when he was out of the house. The evening had felt charged, John relishing in the thrill of what had transpired on the telephone, combined with the excitement of hanging out with Alex, in Alex's room.

When the buzz had started to die down, John tried to start it up again. "That was crazy, eh? When she realized it was stuffed animals."

Alex delicately dropped the needle on a record and turned in John's direction. But he wasn't looking at John. He was staring past him. "But she didn't realize it."

"What do you mean?"

"It wasn't Mitra who realized it was stuffed animals. It was you who told her it was."

"But," John started. "But she knew there were animals."

"Could have been a lucky guess."

"I don't think so."

"But it could have been. Lots of people have pets. Maybe she was just banking on you having one."

John felt like it was slipping from his grasp, the wonder of the psychic reading, his connection with Alex. "But she said there were lots of animals!"

"I don't know," Alex said, wariness in his voice. "If you really think about it—"

"Well, then," John interrupted, "why were you listening to the show if you don't believe it?"

"Because it was funny," Alex replied, annoyed. "Because I had nothing better to do. Geez, John, why do you have to be such a fucking spaz?"

I don't have to be one because I'm not one, John thought, lying in the grass on top of the hill. The question he wanted answered was why Alex thought it was okay to be friendly one minute, and then turn around and be vicious the next. And he wanted to know why there were so few friendly moments nowadays.

High overhead, an airplane came into view. John held out his right arm, and made his hand into a fist. He stuck out his forefinger and lined it up with the back end of the airplane's tail. He followed its progress, keeping his finger right behind the tail, and imagined he was pushing the airplane across the sky.

On Mondays, there was a gathering before first bell around a bench in the upper foyer at school. Alex's friend Kurt called it the Monday Morning Broadcast. The bench was installed in the floor before an immense window that overlooked the back of the school, with a view of the gravel running track that surrounded the soccer field, the goals with no nets, the white goalposts dotted with rust, and the copse of trees at the edge of the grounds that kids disappeared into to smoke. There were other, identical, benches in the foyer, but the Broadcast always took place on this bench. There was room on it for six – seven or eight if those seated were feeling particularly generous with their personal space – while the rest of the gathering stood around or sat on the floor.

This was the realm of the popular boys in Grade Eleven. On Monday mornings, they recounted and rehashed stories of conquest, mayhem, and inebriation from the recent weekend. There was nothing Alex loathed more. And there was nothing he was more scared to miss.

He stood in the circle of kids surrounding the bench, his hands in the pockets of his jeans, trying to look, trying to feel, like he belonged. Kurt was standing right next to him but, somehow, on the periphery, his hands also thrust into the pockets of his baggy khakis, looking bored and annoyed. Their connection, their way in with this particular group of boys, was their friend Eric, who was seated on the left edge of the coveted bench. In years past, it had just been Alex, Kurt, and Eric – Kurt liked new wave, Eric liked punk, and Alex liked both. All three had an affection for *Star Trek*, a kind of fondness that allowed them to delight in the program while laughing at it a tender way; and though not one of them could play a note, they often spoke of starting a punk band, which they'd name The Coprophagics, a word Alex had inadvertently (and happily) come across in the big dictionary in the school library.

But, starting back in September, Eric had drifted into the circle of popular boys. This development was the upshot of Eric's summer job as a busboy in the clubhouse at the Montclair Golf Club. One of the boys from the bench, Barry Hill, also worked there. Eric came back to school with an affinity for pot, parties, and a different crowd. He never broke off his friendship with Alex, and there were still sporadic flashes of the old Eric (occasions limited to when the two were alone or with Kurt), but Alex knew an ugly transformation had taken place. Among Eric's new friends, Alex and Kurt were mostly ignored and yet tolerated; they were not invited to the parties but, Monday mornings, they were invited to hear all about them. For Alex, this role as an audience member was excruciating; he yearned to participate. He also yearned to smash all of their faces with a brick.

"So Barry went into the bedroom with Valerie," Matt Waite said from the centre of the bench. All eyes turned to Barry, seated next to Matt. From somewhere, an approving voice said, with relish, *Yeah.* "And we were, like, totally checking it out."

"You guys are fucking peeping toms," Barry said with a big smile on his face.

"Language!" Mr. Holt, the principal, was walking by the bench along with Albert, the school janitor. Holt's voice elicited a muted chorus of snickers. He stared at the crowd, his eyebrows arched in anger, but didn't stop walking. He continued with Albert to the wall outside the adjoining hallway, where he pointed out some rather large graffiti that had been recently drawn with black marker: the letters V and D inside of a diamond. The janitor made a fruitless attempt to wipe the markings from the wall with a rag. Mr. Holt took the rag from the janitor and tried washing the wall himself, also to no result.

Eric took up the story from Matt. "So Barry and Valerie were in there and we had the door open on a crack," he chortled, "but they didn't know." Alex realized the addition of this detail was more important for Eric than for the story. Rather than add colour to the tale, the statement's purpose was to make it known that Eric had been at the scene, too. For Alex, the superficiality was repugnant. But, he knew, he was equally shallow for simply standing there; by hanging around the bench he hoped it would be assumed, by those milling about in other parts of the foyer, that he had been a part of whatever it was that was being so joyfully discussed.

As the party story continued to unfold, Kurt nudged Alex's arm with his elbow. He turned from the bench and motioned with his head. "Come on," he said, taking one step away. "Let's go somewhere else."

Alex shook his head slightly and, adopting the affected noncha-lance Eric now used with him, said, "Nah."

Alex's first class of the day was French. It had long been his weakest subject and, thanks to passing Grade Ten French by only the slimmest of margins, he now found himself in the remedial class. Everyone called it Bobo French. This included the kids in Bobo French them-selves, who used the term with mock pride. Alex took part in the self-ridicule, too. After closing his locker, flanked by Eric and Kurt, he gar-bled and slowed his speech, announcing, "Me go to Bobo Fwench now. Bye-bye fwends." How could they laugh at him when he was already laughing at himself?

The teacher was Monsieur Baron, a serious-looking, grey or beige suit-wearing man in his mid-fifties. He had a monk's hairline; what hair he had left was salty grey, and the cap of exposed skin atop his head was shiny beneath the classroom lights. He wore rounded glasses with thin, barely visible frames. His demeanour was businesslike; his job was to get his students the Grade Eleven French credit they needed for a high-school diploma. Monsieur Baron didn't love his class's nick-name but appreciated the humour in it. "*Vous n'êtes pas des bobos,*" he declared, with passion, on the first day of Grade Eleven. "Bobos," he went on, "are the students who fail my class."

The class was populated by a cross-section of the school; there were jocks, nerds, stoners, and preps. There was Rodney Markus, a kid who was new but not really because he'd lived in Montclair when he was little before moving to California. Now he was back and hard-ly remembered any French. There was Mikey Lefort, perfectly bilin-gual with a French dad and an English mom, who was placed in Bobo French after smoking and snoozing his way to a D-minus in Grade Ten. The largest group in the class was made up of rockers; there was no shortage of jackets of denim or leather, tight jeans, construction boots or white running shoes with the laces undone, and heavy metal T-shirts. Whether it was feathered, layered, or flat, girls and boys alike wore their hair long. Glancing around the classroom back on the first day in September, Alex had felt alone and not a little aloof. He knew who all of these kids were, he just didn't *know* anybody.

Monsieur Baron didn't allow social divisions to determine the seating arrangements in his classroom. To encourage mixing, he imposed assigned seats and changed them regularly. So, on that Monday morning, when Alex walked into class, Monsieur Baron was waiting by the door, and pointed him to a new seat. The same went for every student who walked in after him. That was how Alex ended up with a desk next to the rocker Tina Robinson.

Tina put her elbows on her new desktop and leaned forward, resting her chin in her hands. Her long blond hair was exceedingly teased, and fell around her face like a lion's mane. A tuft of wavy, hair-sprayed bangs swept across the left side of her forehead. She wore earrings in the shape of crosses, and around her left wrist were half a dozen plain, thin bracelets, the colour of stainless steel. Her jeans were faded blue, with a hole in one knee. Her Stan Smith sneakers had once been white, but were now a foggy grey, and speckled with little nicks and scratches.

"What." Tina snapped. She'd caught Alex staring.

"Nothing." He pretended to be offended. But it was her jean jacket he was looking at. The way she'd decorated it herself, in black marker, with the names of bands. Not just their names but perfect reproductions of each group's distinctive, trademark lettering from album covers and posters. All over the back of the jacket and down the sleeves: Iron Maiden, Metallica, Mötely Crüe, Scorpions, Slayer, Ratt, Judas Priest, Dokken, Twisted Sister, and still more Alex hadn't had time to register before being forced to look elsewhere.

Monsieur Baron asked the class to take out their books, a novella they'd been reading aloud for a few weeks called *La Dynamite*. It told the story of a ramshackle town at the base of a tall mountain whose rather large population of unemployed men – the book called them *vagabonds* – gathered daily in the town square to drink, commiserate, and drink some more. One day, a convoy of jeeps arrived in town, escorting a large transport truck with a payload of dynamite, destined for a mining operation on the other side of the mountain. Aware that the road ahead was treacherous and, in some places, snowed in, the company needed to hire some temporary, extra hands to get the dynamite delivered. Spurred by the prospect of good drinking money for a few days' work, the vagabonds vied for a spot on the crew. A dangerous trek ensued.

The funny part was Monsieur Baron's insistence on the proper pronunciation of the word *vagabond* in French, which appeared at least once in nearly every paragraph of the book. He particularly emphasized the word's third and final syllable, describing and demonstrating, time and again, class after class, how the students should shape their mouths and position their tongues in order to produce the correct long *o* sound, followed by the silent *n* and *d*.

Monsieur Baron called on Rodney, the California kid, to read first. He struggled on his initial try with *vagabond* and fell back to pronouncing it the English way.

"Non, non," Monsieur Baron interrupted Rodney's reading. Swirling a finger like an orchestra conductor for each syllable, the teacher sang, "*Va-ga-BOND*." Mr. Baron rose to his tiptoes with lips pursed and eyes wide as he uttered the *bond* part of the word with great flourish, triggering a smattering of laughter.

Rodney tried again, with more success than the first time, but not enough for Monsieur Baron's satisfaction, and the class was treated to a second professorial recital of *va-ga-BOND*. The laughter was louder and more widespread this time, which Monsieur Baron, with an expression of confusion on his face, managed to hush with his hands.

It was Alex's turn to read. He felt giddy for what he was about to do. He began and, two sentences in, encountered the amusing word. As naturally as he could muster, he pronounced *vagabond* in English. Monsieur Baron cut in to help him out. The classroom purred with anticipation. And, when it exploded with howls following Monsieur Baron's third, dramatic performance of *va-ga-BOND* in less than five minutes, Alex caught Tina staring, could feel her eyes on him. He returned her stare. She offered a smile before quickly looking down at her open book. Alex's earlobes tingled with warmth. And while Monsieur Baron struggled to regain control of the boisterous classroom, Alex continued to look in Tina's direction. Finally, she looked up again. Her cheeks were rosier than they had been a moment before.

"Make him say it again," she whispered.


Pizza Dovolos, located between the travel agency and the dry cleaners at the Plaza Montclair strip mall, was a popular spot after school. A loud crowd of teenagers was spilling out onto the sidewalk, blocking the pizzeria's front entrance from view. John pulled up on his bicycle and took in the scene: the laughing, the yelling, the breakdancing, the slices of pizza on grease-stained white paper plates. He wasn't surprised to find the bike stand right outside the restaurant to be full. *Come on, Maximillian,* he thought to the BMX, *I'll find you a safe spot to lock up.*

John coasted down the sidewalk to the Provigo. He slid his bike's front tire into one of the last remaining slots of the bike stand outside the grocery store. *Here's a comfy place.* John patted his bike between the handlebars, and then crouched to lock it. He threaded the chain through the spokes of his front tire, around the rail of the bike rack, over his bike's frame, and around the rail again. He snapped his lock shut and pulled at it to test it. He tested it two more times. *See you soon!*

John could smell the pizzeria some distance from its front door. The scent was even stronger inside, where John's nose was bombarded by a combination of warm baking dough, piquant tomato sauce, and choking cigarette smoke. The front part of the restaurant was dominated by a melamine counter atop a refrigerated glass display case. Behind the glass were lines of soda cans, various juices, and beer bottles. Tammy Dovolos, who was in Alex's grade at school, was taking orders at the cash register. Behind Tammy, through a rectangular cut-out in the wall, was a view of the kitchen, the big pizza oven, and the stainless steel countertops. Tammy's father, Jimmy, wearing a tomato sauce-stained apron and with a cigarette hooked in the corner of his mouth, was slicing a hot pizza with practiced speed.

John turned from the front counter and made his way to the back of the restaurant. He didn't come to Pizza Dovolos for the food; he came to play Gauntlet. Past the rows of tables and chairs, adjacent the bathrooms, lined along the pizzeria's back wall, were four arcade cabinets: Galaxia, Donkey Kong Junior, Super Xevious, and, Jimmy's most recent acquisition, Gauntlet.

Billy, Ralph, and Tony were already there, smoking, waiting for him. All three had long hair, wore tight jeans, white running shoes, and blue jean jackets. Billy, wearing a Dio T-shirt beneath his unbuttoned jacket, nodded in his direction. John glanced at the other two. Ralph had an Iron Maiden T-shirt and the moustached Tony's was Accept. They were rockers from Alex's grade. John had been playing Gauntlet with them after school since early March, when, after a couple of weeks of playing Donkey Kong Junior by himself, he'd finally worked up the guts to ask the trio if he could join them as the fourth player in their game. They were only too happy to oblige, as long as John was willing to be Thyra, the only female character in Gauntlet, keeping Thor, Questor, and Merlin for themselves. John didn't mind. He just wanted to try Gauntlet. And, besides, in the artwork on the side of the machine, Thyra wielded a cool sword and shield.

There was also an inexplicably sexy feeling that John got from playing Thyra. As he navigated her through the mazes, collecting keys and fighting off monsters and ghosts, it was almost as if he was his own girlfriend.

The four of them played until they collectively ran out of quarters. "Let's go smoke one out back," Billy said, tucking his long, dark hair behind his ears with the fingers of both hands. "You coming, John?"

"No, thanks."

"*Just say no,*" Tony snorted.

"I wouldn't let you smoke up anyway," Billy said with great seriousness. "Your brain cells are way too precious. But come with us. There's something we want to show you. Well, actually, something we want you to listen to."

There was a narrow delivery lane behind the strip mall. Old crates, garbage bags, and sodden cardboard boxes lined the back wall between each of the stores' back doors. A concrete retaining wall ran the length of the lane opposite the back of the building. A slender strip of yellowed grass grew along the top of the wall, bordered by a chain-link fence. Billy hopped up on the wall and walked along the grass. Tony and Ralph did the same. John kept walking in the lane. They came to a section of fence that was broken, lying flat on the ground. "You coming?" Billy called to John. He offered a hand and John clasped it. He was hoisted onto the wall. He followed the rockers through the opening, his feet springing slightly on the trampled portion of fence.

They were in a field of long grass that was as tall as John's thighs. The dandelions grew tall, too, and scraggly bushes were scattered about. In the middle of it all was a solitary maple tree with a thick trunk and a lush head of branches. John passed the tree as he followed the rockers deeper into the field. He listened to the drone of cicadas. The three older boys stopped when they came upon a collection of abandoned tires. Tony and Ralph sat on two of the tires, where Tony began to meticulously roll a joint. Billy unclipped his Walkman from the waistband of his jeans and handed it to John. "Check this out." John read the handwritten label on the tape inside: *Vile Druids.* "It's our band," Billy said. He raised his left fist and held it in front of John's face. Scrawled on the back of Billy's hand in black marker was a logo John had been seeing around school of late: the letters V and D inside a diamond. "We recorded a new song this weekend."

"What's it called?" John asked.

Billy's eyebrows arched and he frowned slightly. "We just made it. There's no title yet."

"Vagabond!" Tony called out suddenly. He pronounced the word in French.

Billy's expression changed in an instant. A wide smile came across his face. "Yes! Vagabond!" he laughed and tapped the Walkman with his finger. "It's called '*Vagabond.*'"

John placed the headphones over his ears and, while the other three smoked their joint, he explored the field, the loud and raw sounds of the Vile Druids chugging in his ears. Over the tape hiss came a relentless charge of electric guitar, some adequate drumming, and the incomprehensible vocals of a growling monster, apparently Billy. John came to a section of the field where the grass was even taller than the rest, growing to his waist. He waded through it, discovering more tires strewn about, along with some overturned shopping carts from the Provigo, and a stainless steel kitchen sink. John stopped and turned around. He could no longer see the back of the strip mall.

When he rejoined Billy, Ralph, and Tony, the rockers were quiet and tired looking, sitting on tires. The murky scent of pot hung in the air.

"So," Billy said. "What do you think?"

"It's really cool," John replied, handing the Walkman back.

"You play an instrument?"

"Piano. A little bit."

"We don't need a piano player."

"I have a mouth harp."

"You have a what?"

"A mouth harp." John brought both of his hands to his mouth and mimed playing the mouth harp.

The rockers looked at each other, their stoned eyes opened wide now. "A *mouth harp!*" Tony shouted.

Billy fiddled with his Walkman and popped the tape out. "Here," he said, gesturing with it at John. "For you. It'll be worth a million bucks one day."

"Thanks," John said. "See you guys tomorrow." He picked his way back to the downed fence section and, passing through it, heard Tony cry out again.

"A *mouth harp!*"

John hopped down from the retaining wall and jogged out of the delivery lane, back to the front of the strip mall. He unlocked his bike and started riding, thinking about what it might be like to be in a death metal band. As he got closer to home, his thoughts turned to Mitra, and how he was looking forward to hearing her show again on Friday night. Alex's doubts about her also crossed his mind. There had to be a way to prove her powers true.

The garage door was open; the oil-spotted cement floor and the dusty shelves filled with old gardening pots, mildewed books, and cast-off board games were visible from the driveway. John rode into the garage and got off his bike. He parked it next to Alex's ten-speed, propped on its kickstand in the back of the garage. He patted his BMX on the handlebars and seat, then closed and locked the garage door.

For the rest of the week, John's after-school ritual remained the same. But on Friday after Gauntlet, instead of parking his bike in the garage as usual, John rode it around the side of the house to the back yard. He got off and walked it across the grass to the far end of the yard, toward the shed. Between the rear exterior wall of the shed and the cedar hedge that bordered the property he found a slice of free space. John slid his bike into the space, leaning it against the wall. "Don't worry, Maximillian," he said, "This is for a good cause."

Alex invited him to listen to *Psychic Radio* in his room again that night. John told his brother he'd come, but not right at the beginning of the show. He stayed in his own room with the telephone. He was Mitra's first caller. She was overjoyed to hear from him again. She said he was her all-time favourite teenager. "And what can we do for you this week, John?"

"Um," he began, "I lost my bike."

"Your bike? Oh, no. Oh, John. I can tell this bike is very important to you."

"*Very* important," John replied. His heartbeat increased in speed and he felt a little queasy. He didn't like to lie. But Alex needed to be convinced.

"Let me think on this a bit, John. Let me think... let's see... okay... okay... John?"

"Yes?"

"Do you think your bike has been stolen?"

"Um, well, no, I don't know. I don't think so." John felt sweat forming on his brow. "I think it's only lost. Not stolen."

"Okay, John, I'm seeing something, but it's not really clear. Something is clouding it. But I'm seeing a house."

"A house?"

"Yes. A house."

"A small house?"

"It could be a small house."

"Like a shed?"

"A shed...oh, yes! A shed! John, I think your bike is in a shed."

"Or behind it?"

"Or behind one. It *could* be behind a shed."

"I'm going to look behind our shed! Thank you!"

John hung up the receiver and darted from his room. Maximillian had been left out in the open long enough. In his bare feet, John ran out to the back yard and dragged his BMX from behind the shed. He walked it into the garage.

Alex was waiting for him. "What is going on?"

"I lost my bike," John said. "Did you hear? Mitra found it."

"Yes, I heard it. But how do you *lose* your bike behind the shed?"

"Mitra knew where it was."

"You *told her* where it was. And you put it there yourself, didn't you?"

John looked at the concrete floor of the garage, cold beneath his feet.

"Why are you such a spaz?" Alex asked.

The Bobo French class was assigned an interview project: in groups of two, each student had to ask the other three questions. The partners were to work out their questions and answers in advance of presenting their interviews in front of the whole class. And, the partners were selected by the teacher. When the class groaned at this announcement,

Monsieur Baron looked genuinely surprised. What would be the point, he asked, of interviewing someone you already know?

Alex's belly stirred when Monsieur Baron paired him with Tina. A prickling broke out behind his ears and on the back of his neck. It was exactly what he'd been hoping for.

Trying to act cool, he turned to Tina and said, "So I guess we're stuck with each other."

"Wow. You seem so overjoyed."

"No," Alex replied quickly, feeling idiotic. "It's fine. Sorry. It's totally fine."

Tina smoothed her sweeping band of bangs with her hand. "Why don't we make this easy? You tell me three things about you and I'll tell you three things about me. Then we'll come up with the questions. I was born in Sherbrooke, I live in the Normandie Apartments, and..." Tina paused. Her eyes searched the room. She suddenly looked inspired. She grabbed the lapels of her jean jacket with both hands and opened it. She motioned with her chin at the Judas Priest baseball shirt she wore beneath it. "And I like metal. Obviously."

"It's not *that* obvious," Alex teased. "I mean, doesn't everybody draw the logos of, what, thirty heavy metal bands on their jackets?"

With some pride, Tina glanced down at her jacket. "Sure they do," she said, looking at Alex again. "So, where's yours?"

"I left it at home today."

"Of course you did." Tina was smiling now. "But seriously, what kind of music do you listen to?"

"Punk. Hardcore." Alex couldn't bring himself to say new wave.

"Yeah, right."

"I'm serious."

"You don't look like a punk."

"And you don't look like a metal head."

"You're a real comedian."

"No, I'm a punk, remember?"

The bell rang. Without any warning, Tina reached out and grabbed Alex's left wrist. Holding it firmly, she wrote on his forearm with her pen. It tickled.

When she was done, her telephone number was on his skin.

"Let's work on the project tonight over the phone," Tina said. She stood up from her desk. "Call me. But after nine."

When she was safely out the classroom door, Alex grabbed his own pen and copied Tina's phone number down on the inside cover of his binder. He then used the pen to blot her handwriting on his arm, replacing it with a messy blue smudge, before any of his friends could see it there and ask whose number it was.


That night, as the clock crept closer and closer to nine o'clock, an ache, somehow pleasant, materialized inside Alex's stomach. He brought the telephone from the living room to his own room, dragging the cord behind him, and closed his door. So as to not appear as eager as he was feeling, he waited until three minutes past nine to dial Tina's number.

She answered on the second ring.

"Hi, Tina? It's Alex. You know, your friend from Bobo French class?"

"Very funny. I think I know where you're *from*, Alex."

"I didn't want there to be any confusion. You might know several people named Alex."

"You're the only one."

"I'm special! I'm special!"

"*Special* certainly describes you."

"Well, I'm in a special class, aren't I?"

"Speaking of which," Tina said, adopting a more businesslike tone, "did you come up with questions for my answers?"

"Yes. But I have one more."

"Three is the limit."

"This one's not for the assignment. Why did you make me wait until after nine to call?"

"Because I'm busy until nine."

"Busy doing what?"

"Hanging out with my dad, if you must know."

"Oh."

"He leaves for work at nine."

"He works at night?"

"Some people do, you know."

"I didn't mean anything by it."

"Sorry. Some people think it's weird."

"That he's a prostitute?"

"Very funny. If you must know, he works at the Sheraton in Laval. He does the night shift at the reception desk."

"So, it's just you and your mom at night?"

"My mom's, um, not around."

"Oh. Sorry."

"She's not *dead*. She's just not around. Never really was."

"So, you're alone?" Alex asked. "Every night?"

"I am indeed."

"What do you do?"

"What do you mean what do I do?"

"I mean, you can do whatever you want. What do you do?"

"Um, my homework. Watch TV. Listen to records."

"That's *it*?"

"Well, tonight I'm planning on making a bowl of Jell-O."

Alex couldn't understand how Tina could be so blasé about being left alone at night. There was nothing he would like more than to have the house to himself every night. Or, for that matter, for just one night.

They continued talking, about anything but their French assignment. It turned out Tina had been to a party the previous Friday night.

"The one at Linda McKean's?" Alex had heard all about it earlier that day, during this week's Monday Morning Broadcast. "How was it?"

"It was a total make-out convention, actually."

Alex felt a bitter stab of jealousy. He hid it by adopting a gossipy tone. "Oh, yeah?"

"Totally. You couldn't even count the amount of people who were making out."

"Sounds wild," Alex said. He squeezed the telephone receiver in his hand and ground his teeth. "So, who did you make out with?"

"I'm sorry?"

"You don't have to be sorry." Alex's tone was cold.

"I didn't say I was sorry. I said I didn't hear you. But, actually, I did hear you. Why would you ask such a question?"

"Excuse me for being curious. *You're* the one who said it was a make-out factory."

"And *you're* the one who asked me about the party in the first place. Look, I gotta go. I have other homework to do."

"But. But we didn't—"

The line went dead.

Alex relaxed his grip on the receiver but kept it to his ear, willing the connection to re-establish itself. Willing time to move backwards two minutes, to before he'd starting acting like a dick.

There was a knock at his door. Alex ignored it. There was another knock, followed by John's soft, infuriating voice calling Alex's name. Alex hung up the telephone and walked slowly toward the door. He stopped before it, and turned slightly to one side. He kicked the door with as much force as he could muster, at the level he imagined John's face would be.

Alex listened to his younger brother's footsteps trail away down the hallway. Then he threw himself onto his bed.

John knew better than to knock at Alex's door a second time; his older brother was obviously in one of his dark moods. But later, when he heard Alex get in the shower, John stole into his room with the Vile Druids cassette, his mouth harp, and a portable tape recorder. He'd been contemplating something for a few days and, like when he worked up the courage to ask the rockers if he could play Gauntlet with them, he finally felt ready to move forward. He just needed Alex's stereo to complete his plan.

Thanks to his secret forays into Alex's room to listen to his records, John knew his way around the stereo. He slipped the Vile Druids tape into one of Alex's cassette decks and set up his own, small tape recorder, already loaded with a fresh blank cassette, on the floor next to one of Alex's speakers. He settled himself in a sitting position on the floor and pressed the PLAY and RECORD buttons on his tape recorder. He pressed the PLAY button on Alex's stereo, and raised his mouth harp to his lips.

Billy, Ralph, and Tony's song started up, and John plucked out a repeating melody to accompany it. His bottom gums went dry after only a minute, but he kept going, even near the end, when they felt on the verge of cracking. When the song finished (with ten seconds of heavy breathing, courtesy of Billy), John stopped his tape recorder, popped the Vile Druids tape out of the stereo, and crept out of Alex's room. As he passed the bathroom, he heard the water turning off in the shower.

In his own room, John played back his enhanced version of "Vagabond." The guys are going to love this, he thought.

Hair wet, a damp towel wrapped around his waist, Alex returned to his room. He had been humming Minor Threat songs in the shower, and now he slipped the *Out of Step* album from his stack of albums. Record in hand, he turned to his stereo and was surprised to find one of his cassette decks open. As he pressed it shut, he had an idea.

A genius of an idea, he thought.

The next morning before first bell, instead of joining Eric and the other boys assembled around the bench in the upper foyer, Alex passed them by without stopping.

"Where the fuck is *he* going?" Alex heard Barry Hill ask no one in particular.

"Fuck if I know," Eric replied.

Like they actually care, Alex thought.

He continued on down the hall, weaving in and out of clusters of morning gatherings before the rows of lockers. Voices buzzed all around him. He passed the janitor, who was painting over a new patch of VD graffiti on the wall next to the entrance to a boys' bathroom. The cosmetology and shop classrooms were at the end of the hall, and many of the rockers were known to have their lockers in the area. Alex spotted the back of Tina's jacket in the crowd and made his way toward her. She was talking with a friend, a girl with long, dark feathered hair, wearing a black leather jacket and grey jeans. Alex circled around the friend and came up behind her, placing himself in Tina's sightline.

"Um, hi," he offered.

"Hello." Tina's tone was indifferent. She stared at him with an exaggerated look of expectation on her face.

"Can I, um, talk to you for a sec?"

"You don't have to ask permission."

Alex forced out a little laugh and cast a quick glance at Tina's friend. She got the hint and muttered, "I think I'll leave you two alone." She drifted away.

Alex looked at the floor and cleared his throat. His heart was beating so hard and so fast, he could feel it in his ears. "I'd like to apologize," he began, looking up at Tina, "for being a jackass on the phone last night."

Tina's expression remained unchanged.

"I shouldn't have asked what I asked. I don't know why I did it. It just came out." He wanted to go on. He wanted to tell her he knew very well why he had asked. He wanted to tell her he had asked because he was dying to know if she'd been with someone at the party. He wanted to tell her he wanted to know all of this because he wanted to be with her. But all he could muster was, "So, I'm sorry."

Tina's face softened. "I thought you were brave when I saw you in this end of the school. But, after that, I think you're really brave. Thanks for saying sorry."

"Oh!" Alex blurted out. He reached into the back pocket of his jeans and pulled out a cassette case. He gave it a little shake, rattling the tape inside. "I almost forgot. I made this for you."

"For me?" Tina extended both of her hands. Alex deposited his gift into her palms. "What for?"

"It's, like, an *I'm sorry* present, I guess. I made it for you last night after we got off the phone. There isn't any metal on it, but I put some stuff on there that's pretty fast."

Tina feigned horror. "Oh, no. No *metal*? I didn't know other music even *existed*."

Alex watched Tina turn the cassette case over in her hands. He glanced back and forth between her eyes and his own handwriting on the title card he'd filled out with the names of the songs and artists he'd put on the tape.

The bell rang for first period.

"If you can't handle the lack of metal, at least listen to the first song I put on there. You'll like the title." He took a step closer to Tina and placed the pad of his index finger on the cassette case, pointing to "Tina" by Camper Van Beethoven.

His hand was so close to hers.

"Oh, cool!" Tina sang with genuine enthusiasm. "Thanks!"

Alex was late getting to Economics. He accepted the tardy slip with pleasure.


Billy, Ralph, and Tony were waiting for John by the Gauntlet machine after school. John's head was swimming in the giddy thrill of anticipation but, as he studied the serious expressions on the rockers' faces, the feeling quickly changed to remorse and dread. How could he have so badly misinterpreted their excitement over his mouth harp? The three older boys moved toward John as he approached the back of Pizza Dovolos, stopping him in his tracks. They stared straight at him, intensity in their slightly bloodshot eyes. John was sure he had offended them with his recording. He felt the first little sprinklings of tears welling in his eyes. A few months ago, the sadness that was building inside would have been over the end of his chance to play four-person Gauntlet every day. Now it was over the end of three friendships.

The rockers stood over John – they were so much taller than him. Billy broke the silence. "We're not playing Gauntlet today."

"Okay," John choked out, accepting his fate. He looked at his feet.

"We're playing music today!" Billy shrieked in his best death metal voice.

Up at the front of the restaurant, Jimmy Dovolos poked his head out from the kitchen and yelled, "Hey! Quiet down back there!"

Billy waved a dismissive hand in Jimmy's direction. He turned back to John. "Seriously, man. What you did was amazing!" He glanced at his two bandmates. Ralph reached out and patted John roughly on the shoulder. Tony flashed him a toothy smile and lit up a cigarette. Billy continued, "Dude, we've talked about it. The vote was unanimous. You're in the band. I mean, if you accept. You're a Vile Druid!"

John could not respond immediately. He had to rein in his happy, happy thoughts. He could see the guys were waiting for him to say something. He opened his mouth, coughed at Tony's cigarette smoke, and said, "I do."


That night, after nine, on the telephone, Tina had some feedback for Alex about his tape. "You definitely have interesting taste in music."

"I'll take that as a real compliment coming from a rocker."

"Shut up," Tina laughed. "I liked the Black Flag, but I'd heard it before. I liked the Vandals, and, wait, let me look at it. Oh, yeah. I liked The Smiths, too, believe it or not. But the one I really liked was that song, 'Back in Flesh.'"

"Wall of Voodoo."

"What a voice."

"Stan Ridgeway."

"*Well you can't tell ME what to do.*"

"*You can't tell me what to* do."

"*Fuck you.*"

They both laughed at their impromptu duet.

"And what about the first song?" Alex asked.

"I must say, I like the title."

"I thought you would."

"With a name like Camper Van Beethoven, I really didn't know what to expect. They sound like a bunch of weirdoes. Are they European?"

"They're from California. Maybe they're surfers who smoke a lot of pot."

"What about you?" Tina asked.

"What about me what?"

"You ever smoke pot?"

"Sure," Alex lied.

"Then maybe you can help me."

Alex swallowed. A queasy feeling came over him.

"There's something I've always wanted to know," Tina said. "Is it true that smoking up makes you hungry?"

Alex cleared his throat. "That's what they say," he began, "but that's not what happened with me." He thought that sounded pretty good. "Wait," he said. "You mean, you've never tried it?"

"Nope."

"I thought—"

"You thought because I dress the way I dress and because I listen to the music I listen to, that I was a stoner?"

"Maybe not necessarily a *stoner...*"

"You're such a dick," Tina teased. "And anyway, look at us. Out of the two of us, only one person's smoked pot. And it's not the metal-head."

Alex immediately regretted not telling the truth to Tina. Was it possible, he wondered, that fabrications and poses were simply not necessary to connect with Tina?

There was to be a party on Friday night, Tina told Alex, at Katarina George's house. Her parents were off to Cuba for a week.

"How do you get parents like that?" Alex grumbled.

"What do you mean?"

"I mean, how can I get myself some parents like that, who go away for a week. My mother can't go to the mall without calling home to check on me."

"My dad used to call a lot, when he first started the night shift. But after a while, and after waking me up for no good reason, he stopped."

"That's what I don't get about you: you can pretty much do whatever you want but you don't do anything. If I was left alone every night, I'd be... I'd be..."

"You'd be what?"

"I don't know. Walking the streets, going places."

"You don't even know what you want."

"I want to go to that party."

"So, come."

"Even if I managed to get out of the house, I'm not even invited anyway."

"What do you mean you're not *invited?*"

"I mean exactly that. I'm not invited."

"Nobody gets *invited* to parties. You just show up. Do you think there's a guard at the door? Who's not going to let you in?"

"Okay," Alex declared, "if you go, I'll go. I'll figure out a way to get past my parents."

"Yay!" Tina cried. And in the same, joyous tone sang, "*You can't tell me what to do!*"

On the other end of the line, Alex smiled and listened to Tina laugh and breathe.

The next day in French class, Alex noticed a new addition to Tina's jean jacket. In a space between Dokken and Ratt, the words Wall of Voodoo now appeared. He felt a pleasant burst of chill on the back of his neck.

"I see you've been busy," he quipped. "Wall of Voodoo?"

Tina smiled. "A tribute to Stan."

"You're the coolest."

"Now we have to get you into some metal."

"Make me a tape."

"I might just do that."

When the bell rang, they left the classroom together. Once in the hallway, however, they went their separate ways. Alex wondered if Tina felt the difference outside Monsieur Baron's classroom, too. Inside, social walls didn't exist. Everyone in Bobo French was after the same thing, a Grade Eleven French credit, to graduate. There was no shame among Bobos. But outside, everyone played their assigned roles. He'd felt uneasy, and he'd felt the unease of others, when he'd walked down to the rockers' end of the hallway to give Tina the mix tape. Now he wanted to hang out with her all the time. If only he had the guts to.

Alex spent the lunch hour among the gang in the upper foyer. He didn't talk much to anyone, and the others didn't talk very much to him. He wondered where Tina was, and longed to be with her. He envied Kurt, who hardly showed his face in the foyer anymore. He didn't know where he was hanging out but, wherever it was, whatever he was doing, he admired his resolve.

When the bell rang, he went to his locker to retrieve his books. Eric followed soon after, and dug into his own locker, right beside Alex's. They didn't address each other. Kurt was nowhere to be seen.

Alex's head was in his locker when he heard Eric begin to emulate an electric guitar with his voice, a heavy metal beat. He glanced at Eric, who made a big show of playing air guitar. He gestured with his chin at something behind Alex.

Alex poked his head around his open locker door. He saw Tina and three of her rocker girlfriends walking down the corridor toward them. Eric's guitar sounds grew louder and more intense as the girls drew nearer. In a panic, without stopping to think, Alex turned slightly and backed himself inside his locker, ducking his head to fit beneath the top shelf, and squeezing his shoulders in on his neck in the cramped space. He reached out with one hand and closed the door part-way, just enough for him to hide behind.

A moment later, the door slammed completely shut.

"Hey!" Alex called out in the darkness.

"Fucking spaz!" Eric taunted from the other side of the door.

Alex pushed at the door, to no avail. Eric was laughing his head off out in the hallway. "See ya!" he called.

Alex was abandoned, marooned inside his locker. He had, however, managed to avoid a meeting between himself, Tina, and Eric. Through the slats in the locker, he could make out Tina and her friends passing by, unaware of his presence.

He stood still inside the gloom of his locker, the only light coming from the thin slats. He wanted to get out but he didn't want to call out. To be humiliated. He waited for Eric to come back.

He *would* come back...?

There was a buzz of activity outside in the hallway: chatter, laughter, the opening and closing of other lockers. Soon the bell rang, and the chatter dropped in volume until silence prevailed. Alex made his hands into fists and thumped the interior walls of his locker on either side of him.

He resigned himself to being stuck inside the locker for the entire period. He'd listen for Kurt after the next bell; he would let him out. Alex would have to figure out some way to explain skipping History to his parents once the school got around to informing them. He could have really done without his mother's I'm-so-disappointed-in-you act, but enduring it seemed inevitable.

Alex heard footsteps coming down the hall. The slats before his face darkened, blocking out the light. A voice whispered, "Are you still in there?"

"Tina?"

"Should I call the fire department?"

"How did you know I was here?"

"I saw."

"Thanks for coming."

"What's your combo?"

Revealing his locker combination to Tina felt like such an intimate act.

The locker door opened to brilliant light, and to Tina. She took a step back to allow Alex to step outside. He looked right into her eyes, and she returned the stare. His heart beat rapidly and, as if pulled by a force outside of himself, he drew closer to Tina. He cocked his head to one side. She closed her eyes. He followed suit and sought out her lips with his. The air around him felt electric.

There was a shout, an angry one. "Hey!" The spell broken, Alex opened his eyes. It was Principal Holt, followed by the janitor, carrying another can of paint and a brush. "You two! Get back to class!"

Alex stepped backwards, away from Tina. "See you later," he said.

"Make it sooner," she answered before turning away.

Friday morning, John sprang from his bed before his alarm clock rang. The early morning sun shone through his window, bathing his room in bright light. He was anxious to begin the day, his second as a member of the Vile Druids.

He washed, ate, and packed for school long before anyone else in the family managed to leave their bedrooms. To pass the remaining time, John installed himself at the kitchen table with a pad of paper and a pen. He practiced drawing the Vile Druids' logo, over and over, aiming to get the V and the D aligned perfectly inside the diamond. The events of the previous afternoon were fresh in his mind: the guys could not have made him feel more welcome down in the concrete basement at Tony's house. Surrounded by stacks of damp-looking cardboard boxes, there was a drum kit and an old couch in the middle of the room. The Cave, as the guys called it, was the Vile Druids' practice space and makeshift recording studio (equipment for the latter came in the form of a half-decent boom box on the floor, plugged into the wall, but, as Billy said with no shortage of enthusiasm, they would one day upgrade). John took a guitar lesson from Ralph, who proved to be a patient teacher. After playing parts of two songs, the whole affair had come to an abrupt end when Tony's mother came home and, her Zellers name tag still pinned to her wool sweater, kicked them all out of the house.

John stuffed his pad of paper into his backpack. The noise level in the house was rising incrementally as the rest of the family went through their own morning preparations. John decided to get an early start for school, maybe take Maximillian for a ride around the elementary school and up his hill, with the wind in his ears.

He called out goodbye to his parents and, as he backed out the front door, heard Alex start up a conversation with his mother. John found his brother's tone to be a strange and somewhat robotic. Like a robot trying hard to sound human.

"So, tonight I'm going to Kurt's. And I'm sleeping there. At Kurt's."


At school, between first and second period, Alex happened upon Tina in the hallway near the stairwell.

"I'm coming tonight," he announced quickly.

"They're letting you?"

"They think they're letting me do something else, but whatever. I'm coming."

"I'm so happy."

"Me, too."

"Are you about to be attacked?"

"What?" Alex didn't understand Tina's question.

"Are you in some kind of danger?"

"What are you talking about?"

"You always look around the whole time you're talking to me. To the left, to the right, behind you, behind me. Like you're watching out for something. Why do you do that?"

John met the rest of the band for Gauntlet after school, but their get-together ended early on account of Tony's mom.

"She's on his back again," Billy explained. The four of them had left Pizza Dovolos and were traipsing slowly along the sidewalk before the Plaza Montclair storefronts.

"She's always on his back," Ralph added. "*Mommie Dearest.*"

"You guys shut up," Tony snapped. "Do either of you want to go practice at your houses?"

Neither Billy nor Ralph said anything. John remained quiet, too. He hadn't even told anyone in his family he'd joined a band yet. When they got to the bike rack, John stopped and pulled the key to his lock from his pocket. "Well," he said, "have a nice weekend, guys."

"I'm going to have a nice *stoned* weekend," Billy chortled. "See ya, Johnny!"

"Yeah, see ya," Ralph said. "Stay cool."

Tony stopped and, turning toward John, made a fist at the end of his extended arm. John returned the gesture with his own fist. Face to face, John marvelled at the thickness of Tony's moustache. Of the handful of kids in school who had moustaches, Tony's was by far the fullest. When their knuckles touched, Tony made the sound of an explosion with his mouth.

John unlocked his bike and discreetly whispered hello to it. He got on the seat and began to pedal, but instead of heading for the street, he steered his bike around the side of the strip mall and into the delivery lane in the back.

"I've got a very special mission for you, Maximillian. This is going to prove it once and for all. After this, Alex is going to believe in Mitra."

John stopped at the broken place in the fence and got off his bike. He hoisted it up onto the retaining wall, and then climbed onto the wall himself. He walked his bike through the fence opening and into the field beyond it.

He pushed his bike through the brush, heading to where the grass grew long near the solitary maple tree. Grasshoppers bounded all around him. In the shade of the tree, John waded into the tall grass, and laid Maximillian down inside of it. He kicked gently at tufts of grass blades that he'd flattened, making them stand up again, trying to make the area appear undisturbed.

He took a few steps back. He walked a wide perimeter around the tree, peering into the place where his bike was hidden. When he was satisfied he could see no trace of it, he left the field.

A most terrible cramp gnawed at his gut.

He walked home, telling himself all would be well. He would call Mitra during her show. He would tell her his bike was lost again. She would see where it was and tell him it was in the field, and he would go back there with Alex first thing the next morning. Maybe even right away – they could sneak out a window. Maximillian would be there, waiting for him. Nothing would go wrong, he told himself.

By dinnertime, however, John was picturing a great many things that could go wrong. No longer able to stand it, and without waiting for permission, he announced, while running out the door, that he'd forgotten something somewhere and he'd be right back.

He ran all the way to Plaza Montclair, his lungs burning from the exertion. When he got to the strip mall, the sun was low in the sky; the grass and the bushes in the field were a darker shade of green than they had been earlier. John ran into the tall grass, toward the tree.

A cold, helpless feeling came over him. His bike was not where he'd left it. He slapped at the blades of grass with his hands, hoping to find by touch what he couldn't find with his eyes, or hoping he'd just mistaken the spot, anything that meant it was still there. He got down on all fours and frantically crawled around. The grasshoppers thwacked his face.

John stayed down on all fours and, hidden in the long grass, he wept.

Katarina George's house was already packed when Alex arrived. He snaked his way into the living room, into a crowd of chattering kids clutching beer and wine cooler bottles, Guns N' Roses on full blast. He nodded his head at kids whose eyes met his, but he continued to move on, in search of Tina. Alex heard his name being called repeatedly from across the room.

It was Barry Hill. He waved Alex over. He looked genuinely happy to see him. Alex pushed his way to where Barry stood.

"Dude!" Barry's eyes were bloodshot and droopy. "Dude! Have you seen Eric?"

"Haven't seen him," Alex answered.

"Well, when you do, tell him I'm looking for him. He's got a doobie I want to smoke."

Barry drifted away, quickly finding another conversation to join. Alex passed through a doorway, leaving the living room and entering the kitchen. It was a mess, with empty beer bottles and potato chip bags strewn about the countertops and floor. A group of rockers was installed around a wooden table: all were focused on a kid from Bobo French class, Billy, who was bent over the stove, a cigarette between his lips, lighting it on a red-hot element.

When he came away with his smoke successfully lit, he received a mock cheer from his friends. Alex saw Tina sitting at the table.

"Oh my God, you're here," she said. She made her way over to Alex, holding a bottle of beer in her hand.

"I'm here," Alex replied. "I escaped!"

"Cool!" Tina seemed enthusiastic but Alex sensed a bit of discomfort as she glanced over at her friends.

"Where'd you get that beer?" Alex asked.

"They're selling them downstairs," Tina replied. "Come!"

She moved toward a door that opened to a staircase leading down to the basement. The lineup to get downstairs was all the way to the top, spilling into the kitchen. Once Alex and Tina advanced enough to be inside the narrow staircase, the line was further snarled by the stream of kids making their way back upstairs with their beer purchases. There was a lot of shifting and leaning and turning. Alex found himself standing on the same step as Tina and, as they were jostled by the crowd, they came face to face. Alex's breath came quick, and his collarbone flushed with shiver. They were so close Alex couldn't focus accurately on Tina's face; her nose appeared in double. He titled his head and aimed his lips at hers.

Tina put her hands on his shoulders and gently held him back. "Hey," she said, blushing, "you just got here."

"I'm sorry," Alex said.

"Don't be. The party's just starting. We have all night."

A space opened up on the stair below and Tina stepped onto it, backwards, and she stumbled. She pinwheeled her arms while an expression of fear took over her face. Alex reached out with both of his arms and grabbed her around her lower back. He stepped down to her step and pulled her toward him. Their bodies crashed together. Tina's arms embraced Alex around the shoulders.

"Hey, move up!" Someone was shouting at them from the top of the stairwell. Alex and Tina disengaged.

In the basement, the light was orange and dim. The floor was covered in green linoleum tiles with black floral patterns, several of which had come unglued in one corner or another, exposing dust and crumbs against the black subfloor. Larry Delorme and Steve Reno were set up on a couch not far from the doorway, four two-fours of Labatt 50 stacked beside them. They were selling them for two dollars a bottle. Larry and Steve were in Grade Eleven, too, but Alex didn't know them well. Where they got the money to afford that much beer and how they'd managed to actually buy it, at their age, Alex had no idea. To him, it was yet another example of something that came easier to others than to him. He handed over a two-dollar bill, cracked open his beer, and drank. It wasn't even cold.

There was a commotion on the stairs. Kids pushed to the sides and the lineup parted at the bottom. Katarina George emerged from the empty space.

"Alex," she said frantically, angrily. "Your *mom's* on the phone."

Alex didn't react immediately. His shoulders and the back of his neck felt cold, his stomach sick. He turned to look at Tina. She was buying a beer.

"Well, come *on!*"

Alex followed Katarina up the stairs, feeling the stares and hearing the giggles of those that they passed. At the top, the party seemed louder than it had before. Rick Astley's "Never Gonna Give You Up" was playing in the living room. Half a dozen boys, surrounded by a laughing crowd, were dancing to the tune, mock earnestness on their faces. Katarina led Alex to the hallway and motioned him up the carpeted staircase. She opened the door to her parents' bedroom and closed it behind them. Shelly Woodrow was sitting on the edge of the bed holding a telephone receiver, her palm covering the mouthpiece.

"I don't know what your mother wants," Katarina spat in a whisper, "but I *cannot* get in trouble for this. Keep me out of it."

Alex took the receiver in his hand. He had never felt so embarrassed. He knew what was coming from the other end of the line, but he couldn't believe Katarina and Shelly were going to watch him get it. A part of him actually sympathized with Katarina. He understood where her anger was coming from. Here he was, at a party, finally, and his presence was putting everyone else at risk. He brought the receiver to his ear and mouth. "Hello?"

"What took you so long?" His mother sounded frantic. "I've been waiting more than ten minutes!"

"I came as soon as they found me."

"As soon as they *found* you? What is going *on* there?"

Alex glanced at Katarina and Shelly. Their eyes were fixed on him. "I don't know," he said, hoping, somehow, such a vague response would satisfy everyone.

"What do you mean you don't know? How drunk are you? Did you think I was born yesterday? Did you really think you could get away with this? Let me tell you, Kurt's mother is *very* disappointed in you, too. For making me think you were at her house, under *her* care."

"Okay," Alex said, trying to appear calm, to not show any distress to Katarina and Shelly. "I'm on my way home now."

"Whoa, whoa, whoa," his mother said, incensed. "You're not coming home on your own. Your father's already on his way. He left fifteen minutes ago. You're coming home with him!"

Alex handed the receiver back to Shelly, who hung it up on the cradle. Both girls in the room stared at him with impatience. "Well," Katarina finally said, "what's happening?"

Alex did not want to tell Katarina what was happening. He was desperate to get out of the house, to prevent his father from seeing the house, and to prevent anyone in the house from seeing his father. He handed his unfinished beer to Katarina. "I'm leaving," was all he could bring himself to say.

He flew down the stairs, back down to the living room. All around him kids were talking, laughing, and dancing. None of their fathers were on their way to pull them away from their fun. Their night was not ending before it had even begun.

He didn't know if he envied them or hated them.

He wanted to find Tina, to say goodbye, to explain. But his father could show up at any minute – there was no time keep prying eyes from seeing his father picking him up. He had to get outside, to get down the street and away from the house before his father arrived. But Tina would be wondering where he was. And why he'd abandoned her. If it had been possible for his mother to get him on the telephone, he realized, he could do the same with Tina. He would call her at the party after he got home. She wouldn't be missing him for long.

Alex ran out the door and quickly made his way down the street. An approaching car flashed its high beams on and off at him. Alex yanked the back door open and crumbled into his father's back seat.

"What do you think I am, a taxi driver?"

Alex didn't answer. He didn't say a word the whole way home.

John counted the long minutes all evening. He could not take pleasure in anything; not television, not comic books, not toys. Half-an-hour before *Psychic Radio* began, he installed himself in his bedroom with the radio on and his parents' telephone at the ready. He paced the floor. He bit his fingernails. The moment Mitra's mystic theme music began to play, he dialed in.

Mitra began her show with a monologue about astrological opportunities to achieve peace in Central America. She described scenes of horror in places like Guatemala and Nicaragua, death squads and civil wars, suffering people and ravaged landscapes. There was reason for optimism, however: the supernova, visible to the naked eye in the southern hemisphere of the planet earlier in the year, was a symbol of rebirth and hope. It was now up to the people of Earth to make the most of this moment and change Central America's course of misery. Mitra suggested meditation, eating less meat, and sending poetry to politicians through the mail.

While waiting on hold, John listened to the show through the telephone receiver. He felt terrible for causing trouble with his bicycle when there was so much misery in the world. But Maximillian was missing. He just wanted Mitra to get on with the phone calls.


Alex stormed into the house ahead of his father. He stepped through the vestibule, where the hallway opened to the living room. Off to the right was the kitchen, and his mother was sitting with arms folded across her chest in a hard chair at the table. He looked away as soon as he saw her. She remained silent. Alex knew this was supposed to be a form of punishment, as if her silence would somehow cause him pain. He stomped off through the living room.

He grabbed the telephone from the table next to the couch and dragged it into his room. He slammed the door.


"Oh, John! Not your bicycle again!"

"Uh-huh."

"Poor you!" Mitra's tone was so sweet and sympathetic, like a kindergarten teacher tending to a young pupil's skinned knee.

"You're not having very much luck with that bike of yours, are you John?"

"No. No, I'm not."

"Let me see now. Just let me see." Mitra paused for a moment. "Are you sure you have no idea of where it could be, John?"

"No."

"Where was the last place you saw it?"

"In a field. Behind some stores. I left it there, I shouldn't have." John was on the verge of tears. "I left it there and when I went back it was gone."

"A field. Behind stores. Let me see. A field. Behind stores."

"I shouldn't have done it. I'm sorry."

"Oh, John! You don't have to apologize to me! Don't go beating yourself up like that! You wouldn't beat yourself up on purpose, would you?"

"No."

"Of course you wouldn't. You wouldn't deliberately bring yourself pain, would you, John?"

"No."

"But this bicycle business, John, it really has you up a tree, doesn't it?" Mitra paused again, before asking, "Do you know what I mean, John?"

"Um. I'm not sure."

John thought he heard a click on the telephone line.

"Are you still there, John?" Apparently Mitra had heard the click, too.

"I am."

"Okay. Do you know that expression, John? This problem you're having with your bike, it really has you *up a tree.*"

"I'm sorry," John said. "But I've never heard that expression before."

"Think about it, John. What do you think it means to be *up a tree*? You're an intelligent person, I know you are. What do you think of when I say you're up a—"

"What the fuck is this?" Somehow, Alex's angry voice was in John's ear now, coming through the telephone.

"Um," John said. "I'm on the telephone now."

"Then get the fuck off it!" Alex snarled. "Right fucking now!"

"Oh," Mitra said. "John, we're going to have to let you go."

"Wait!" John called. "My bike! I don't understand!"

The quality of the sound in the telephone receiver had changed. No reply came from Mitra. She was no longer on the line.

Slowly, John slipped the receiver onto the cradle. He stepped away from the telephone. He picked up Droopy One from the bed and hugged the stuffed dog with all of his might.


With the receiver squeezed between his shoulder and chin, Alex dialed Katarina George's number. He told himself he was perfectly justified to put an end to John's phone call. Even if John had been talking on the radio, Alex's need for the telephone was more important. What was talk about some invented past life as a German magician or an Egyptian fisherman compared to love? What was it he'd heard Mitra saying? John was up a tree? What kind of crap was that anyway?

A busy signal sounded on the other end of the line.

Alex redialed.

An image of Katarina's house appeared in his mind. The crowded living room, the messy kitchen, the lineup on the stairs going down to the basement. Down where he'd left Tina without even saying good-bye. Word was surely now circulating throughout the house that Alex's mother had called on the phone and that, after speaking to her, Alex had left. With a sinking feeling, he realized his humiliation would be excellent fodder for the Monday Morning Broadcast. Tina would know his disgrace, too, perhaps even by now. He just needed to talk to her, to explain.

The line was still busy. He tried the number another time and, again, busy.

He thought of how he'd tried to kiss Tina. How while she'd refused his advance, she hadn't done so in a way that ruled it out in the future. Even in the very near future. *You just got here*, she'd said. *We have all night.*

At the sound of another busy signal, Alex slammed the receiver down on its cradle.

He left the telephone and walked to his window. Outside, a streetlamp shone its light on a portion of his street. Turning his head to the left, in the direction from which he'd returned from the party in his father's back seat, Alex could see another streetlamp, brightening another section of the road. Another segment of darkness followed, and then another segment of light. He thought of it as a lighted trail back to Tina. Somehow, through the lights, he could feel himself connected to her, from his bedroom to Katarina George's house.

*Please hear me, Tina*, he thought. *Please know that I'm thinking of you. Please know what I think of you.*

John crept away from Alex's closed bedroom door. He'd heard nothing on the other side of it, even with his ear pressed to the wood. The silence provided John with the guts to go back to his room and pick up the phone again. He called the radio station back.

The producer who answered the calls knew it was him. "John?"

"Yes. I'm sorry about what happened. Could I—?"

"Listen, John. You can't get back on with Mitra."

"But it's very important. It's about my bike. I can't wait a whole week to talk to her again."

"I'm sorry, John, but you can't call next week, either. You can't call ever again. We know your number, we can see it when you call. We have to ban you for swearing. It's station policy."

"I didn't swear!"

"It came from your end of the line during your call, John. I'm sorry. It's an automatic ban."

"But, what about my bike?"

"There's nothing I can do. I'm really sorry. I have to let you go now."

The line went dead. John's heart sank. He felt helpless, like he'd been abandoned in the wilderness with his eyes gouged out and his ears cut off.

John drifted to his window. A crescent moon shone in the black sky. He stared at the rounded outline of the darkened portion of the moon. How easy it was to see, this concealed thing in the sky, hundreds of thousands of kilometres away. Maximilian was so much nearer, but impossible for him to see.

*Show me*, he thought. *Please, Mitra. Show me.*


Kurt confronted Alex at their lockers on Monday morning. "Were you *trying* to get me in trouble? My mother still doesn't believe me when I tell her I didn't know anything about it."

"I'm totally sorry," Alex told him. "I wasn't thinking. I just wanted to go to that party."

"So, what happened?"

"I'm grounded. For, like, a month. I've never been grounded before."

Kurt let out a laugh; a short, scoffing laugh. "Not officially."

"What do you mean?"

"You've never been officially grounded," Kurt elaborated, "but you've always *been* grounded. In a way."

For the first time, Alex saw himself as others saw him. A sixteen-year-old kid in a cage.

Kurt opened his mouth to speak again but something caught his attention over Alex's shoulder. Alex noticed and turned around. Tina, in a black Iron Maiden T-shirt, was standing there.

"Hey," she said.

"Oh, hey!" Alex squeaked.

The two stared at each other, silently, for a moment.

"Um," Kurt stammered. "I need to get a book at the library."

Alex watched his friend walk away. "Wait!" he called after him. "Do you know Tina?"

Kurt turned and took a few steps back in Alex and Tina's direction. "Well, I know who she is. I don't really *know* her, though."

"Well," Alex said, "now you know each other."

"Okay," Kurt said, a little shyly. He turned to Tina. "Hi."

"Hi," Tina replied, laughing a little.

Kurt pointed over his shoulder with his thumb. "I have to—"

Left alone with Tina, Alex took a long, deep breath. "I'm really sorry about bailing from the party. I totally got busted."

"I figured as much," Tina said. "Don't worry about it. It was a boring party anyway. Well, it was boring after you left."

"I missed you," Alex forced himself to say, blushing.

Tina stepped forward and, swiftly, pressed her lips to Alex's. He kissed back. He felt a great wave of happiness.

He never wanted it to end.

Tina pulled back slightly. "I have to get to my locker before first bell."

"I'll come with you."

Tina smiled.

To get to Tina's hallway, a walk through the upper foyer was necessary. As the two passed by the gaggle of Alex's friends at the bench, he heard a familiar imitation of an electric guitar coming from the crowd. Alex looked directly at Eric, who, predictably, was the joker behind the music. Some of the other guys joined in, and soon a chorus of mocking guitar sounds filled the foyer.

Alex glanced at Tina. Her face had turned red and her eyes were pointed at the floor. He felt for her hand beside him, and grasped it.

Someone let out a high-pitched whoop. Alex squeezed Tina's hand. She looked up and smiled at him. With his other hand, Alex gave the bench the finger.

Tina suddenly stopped walking. Alex stopped, too, and followed the direction of her stare. Ahead, coming toward them from down the hall, was Billy from Bobo French class. He was walking - being escorted - between the principal and the janitor. Mr. Holt had a hold on one of Billy's arms, cop-like.

"Billy?" Tina said.

Billy had a sour expression on his face. "They think I tagged the walls. I'm going down!"

In the foyer, someone shouted, "Book 'em, Danno!" The boys on the bench laughed and catcalled as Billy disappeared down the stairwell with the principal and the janitor.


"I can't give you any information," Mrs. Dufour said impatiently. "Now go back to class."

"But is it true they're going to be suspended?" John asked. His arms were resting one on top of the other on the shelf before the principal's secretary's window.

"That's none of your concern."

"But will Tony be expelled if he gets one more suspension?"

"That's it," the secretary hissed. "I'm calling Mr. Holt." She pressed one of the transparent buttons at the base of her telephone and grabbed the receiver.

A moment later, Mr. Holt poked his head out from his office door across the hall. "What's going on here?"

A thought materialized in John's mind, an idea, and along with it a quivering sensation in his stomach. He inhaled deeply. He knew what to do.

"I did it!"

"Excuse me?" the principal asked, perplexed.

"I wrote on the wall. I did it! I drew VD all over the place. I'm *in* VD."

Mr. Holt chuckled a little and shared a knowing look with Mrs. Dufour. He cleared his throat and left his office doorway, entering the hall. He approached John and put his large hands on his shoulders. "John, I don't know what's gotten into you, but I hope you don't actually expect me to believe you're the one who's been vandalizing the school."

"It was me," John said. "I did it. I did it all."

"Okay," Mr. Holt sighed. "I think maybe you're trying to be noble. Maybe you're trying to save someone? You're not related to one of those boys, are you?"

"We're all in the same band."

"Band class?"

"No, a *band*. VD – Vile Druids."

Mr. Holt's eyes widened. "I'm sure you are," he said dryly. "Now, I'm going to ask you to go back to class."

"But—"

"Immediately."

Dispirited, John dragged his feet through the lower foyer of the school, heading toward the stairs. He put one hand on the bannister and stopped. Instead of going up to the second floor, to his class, he slunk around the corner of the stairs and into the junior hallway, to his locker. There, from a can where he stored extra pencils and pens, he removed a black marker. He marched straight back to the principal's office.

Mrs. Dufour watched John arrive. She shook her head and blew out a big breath of air from her mouth. She pushed Mr. Holt's button on her telephone.

Unclasping the marker's cap, John took aim at the faux wood of the principal's office door. To Mrs. Dufour's utter disbelief across the hallway, he drew a large diamond on the door. Then, inside the diamond, he wrote the letters V and D.

The door opened. John dropped his marker on the floor.


"I *know* he's your brother, but I can't let you see him. He's in really big trouble." Mrs. Dufour waved at Alex as if to shoo him away. "Now get out of here before you get into trouble, too."

Alex felt angry and helpless. John had never broken a rule in his life, and now rumours were rampant that he was looking at a two-week suspension. "Please listen to me," he pleaded with Mrs. Dufour. "It's impossible that John did this. Impossible!"

"I saw him do it with my own eyes, Alex. With this very pen!" She poked her hand through the opening in her window and slammed a black marker onto the shelf.

Alex looked at the pen, and back at the door with the freshly scrawled Vile Druids logo. He turned back to Mrs. Dufour. "Would you at least let me talk to him?"

"No," she snapped. And, pointing at Mr. Holt's door, added, "He's being dealt with in there. Now, out!"

Alex clasped the marker and backed away from Mrs. Dufour's window. He turned and, working fast, before he could change his mind, drew the Dead Kennedys' DK logo next to John's work.

He returned to a shocked Mrs. Dufour behind her window. He placed the marker back on her shelf. "Now, can I see him?"

Alex and Tina were hiding out in the field behind Plaza Montclair, beneath the solitary maple tree, surrounded by the tall blades of grass. Alex sat with his back against the trunk of the tree, with Tina resting her head on his chest, one arm draped across his collarbone, holding onto his shoulder. "I feel like such a rebel," she quipped, "hanging out with such a vandal."

Alex laughed and hugged Tina closer. "Yeah, well, enjoy it while you can. Once I'm allowed back in school, I won't have any time for you. I'll be too busy breaking windows and kicking over garbage cans."

"Don't forget to pull the fire alarm, too."

"Thanks, I'll save that for after I come back from my next suspension."

"I like this," Tina said.

"You like what?"

"You and me. Being together."

There was a pleasant fluttering about Alex's stomach. He felt happy in a way he had never known was possible. He stared up. In the spaces between the green leaves and the brown branches of the tree, Alex could make out little pieces of blue sky. An airplane, high above, appeared at the edge of one of these pieces and flew across the blue background. It disappeared from Alex's view behind a tangle of tree branches. He shifted his gaze slightly to the side, anticipating the plane's reappearance inside the next open space of the tree.

"What the—?" Alex twisted himself gently from Tina's embrace. He scrambled to his feet. He craned his neck and, still staring above him, took two steps away from the trunk of the tree.

Tina stood, too. She followed Alex's gaze upward. So unusual was the sight, it took a moment for her to understand exactly what it was she was seeing.

A bicycle was up the tree. Its silver frame leaned against the trunk and its tires were held up by two separate branches. It appeared perfectly stable.

"Seriously," Alex said. "What the hell?"

Tina, still looking up, put one hand on the trunk of the tree.

"This is so fucked up," Alex said, mesmerized. "Do you realize whose bike that is?"

Before Tina could even hazard a guess, Alex took her by the hand and started running from the field. "We're going to need help to get it down," he said.

Alex and Tina burst into Pizza Dovolos and jogged to the back of the restaurant where John, Billy, Tony, and Ralph were hunched over the Gauntlet machine. "John!" Alex cried. "John!"

"What?" his brother answered, keeping his eyes on of the game.

"John, your bike! What did Mitra say about it?"

"Nothing," John spat, working his joystick while tapping his MAGIC button. "She didn't have *time* to say anything, thanks to you."

"But she did say something. Don't you remember?"

John glanced at Alex and then back at the game screen. Something about his older brother's appearance made him turn his head again. John saw genuine joy in Alex's face, an expression he'd hardly ever seen him exhibit.

"Well, do you remember or not?" Alex repeated.

"I remember something," John said. "But it didn't make any sense. She said I was up a tree."

"Exactly!" Alex jumped a little in place. "It just hadn't happened yet. But it's going to. Believe me, in about two minutes, you're going to be up a tree!"

Alex reached out and pulled gently at his little brother's arm. "Come with me, John. And bring your friends. You're never going to believe this."

# MY UNCLE, MY BARBECUE
# CHICKEN DELIVERYMAN

The first time I met my uncle Sidney, he pulled a wad of money out of his pocket and laid five bills of different denominations side-by-side on a coffee table. There was a green one-dollar bill, a brownish-orange two, a blue five, a purple ten, and a red fifty. He told me I could pick one to keep.

I chose green.

I don't have any of my own, authentic memories of this event – I was barely two years old when it happened – but the pictures I see in my mind are as vivid as a movie. The story had that much of an impact on me. My mother told it to me when I was seven, while we were packing up our house on Chapleau Street, a few days before we moved to the Normandie Apartments. Cardboard boxes, scavenged from the garbage bin behind the grocery store, were stacked all over the place. My mother had put me to work on the lower levels of a shelving unit we had in the living room, packing books and knickknacks into a box that had once held pineapples.

Tucked in among the books, I found a photo album. It had a burgundy cover that felt like velvet, soft to the touch. I opened it, and flipped through pages filled with pictures of familiar places and faces: my grandparents' house in black and white, the big oak tree in the front yard alongside a second, slightly smaller one that I had only ever known as a stump, and my grandmother and grandfather themselves, younger and less wrinkled. I recognized my mother's face as a child and, in other photos, as a teenager, as well as those of my uncles Morris and Kevin. There were pictures taken in different rooms inside the house, out on the front lawn, and on the shore of the river that was just steps from the yard.

As I went through the photographs, I kept noticing the presence of another child; a third boy. I didn't recognize him, but my mother and my uncles posed with their arms wrapped around his shoulders, laughing beside him, leaning into him.

I called my mother over.

I remember her wearing a light blue bandana with a paisley pattern atop her head, the one she usually tied on when she tackled a big job around the house. A Band-Aid, blackened in spots by dirt, was wrapped around one of her thumbs. I pointed at one of the pictures in the album: a black and white, informal group shot taken on my grandparents' balcony. In the photo, my grandfather was lounging, cigarette in hand, on his chaise longue, surrounded by teenaged versions of my mother, Uncle Morris and Uncle Kevin, and the mystery boy. He was sporting a crewcut, and wore a striped T-shirt and dark, knee-length shorts. I tapped my finger right on the boy's chest. "Who's that?"

After learning of my uncle Sidney's existence and hearing the story of my first and only encounter with him, all I could think about was the fifty-dollar bill I had left on the table. For days, regret weighed down on me. I fantasized about what I could do with such a tremendous amount of money, as if – had I only chosen the red bill – the fifty dollars would have somehow still been at my disposal, unspent, five years later. The toy *Millennium Falcon* in the Consumers Distributing catalogue was going for less than fifty dollars. There'd have been enough left over for action figures.

I formed a link in my mind between Sidney and money. I cast my newfound uncle in the role of the mysterious benefactor, the person who was going to appear again one day and rescue my mother and me.

Sidney would buy me *Star Wars* toys. Sidney would pay for the new catalytic converter our car needed. Sidney would put us back in a real house.

When my thoughts wandered, I would wonder what kind of a person Sidney might be. Was he anything like my other uncles? Morris smoked a pipe, baked luscious vanilla cakes every now and then, and once took me out on his boat for a whole day of fishing. Kevin kept two baseball gloves in the trunk of his car and would invite me to play catch with him out on my grandparents' front lawn. I never even had to ask.

Morris and Kevin both possessed a dry sense of humour, always quick with a joke or a funny retort, and they liked to tease. Growing up, I studied my uncles' style of humour, tried to emulate it, and hoped to be, one day, as amusing as them. They poked fun at their wives, ganged up on my mother, and joined my grandfather at baiting my grandmother, confusing her with absurd questions: "Is it spring forward and fall back? Or is it spring back and fall forward?" Morris stood up from his seat on the balcony and, after making a big show of moving his chair out of the way, demonstrated with great seriousness how it was more natural to fall forward than backward. My grandmother's eyes narrowed with uncertainty. Puffing on her cigarette, she pondered the question out loud for a time (while Morris, Kevin, and my grandfather exchanged mischievous looks). Eventually, she settled on fall forward, only to be immediately talked into fall back by Kevin. Then my grandfather cut in and argued for my grandmother's original choice. They went around and around in this circle until my grandmother, exasperated, sprang from her chair and marched toward the front door. In a wretched tone, she made one last remark before disappearing into the house, an utterance that set the men to whooping: "I don't know what we have to go and change the clocks for anyway!"

There was one particular Sunday visit to my grandparents' house when the usual happy, jocular atmosphere was noticeably absent. This was right after my aunt Christine – Kevin's wife – underwent breast reduction surgery. Everyone spoke softly, and seemed to move about cautiously. The men cast their eyes downward, studying the flaking grey paint on the balcony's floorboards. The women went out of their way to make sure Christine was comfortable – my grandfather even joined in the effort, offering her his chaise longue – but no one even hinted as to why. Several moments of uncomfortable silence passed; the robins in the oak tree provided the only sounds.

Then Kevin diffused the mood.

"So," he quipped, raising both of his hands a little, flexing his fingers, "I guess you all heard I got a hand reduction."

Those Sunday visits to my grandparents' house were an indulgence. Heaping plates of spaghetti, pastries for dessert (and sometimes Morris's cake), cousins to play with in a big yard at the edge of the river, and even though the water was polluted by then the shoreline seemed to me vast: rich with flat skipping stones, croaking bullfrogs hiding in tall reeds, and, after rains, soggy mud that sucked your boots down with satisfying slurping sounds. The apartment my mother and I lived in was cramped. Our little television only got decent reception from three English channels. There was a narrow patch of grass out in front of the building, but it was flanked by a handmade sign on a stake that warned all to keep off it. Though she usually resisted, I asked my mother often about Sidney. I wanted to keep his memory fresh in her mind, to strengthen our tenuous connection to him and to his money. How I wished she would just pick up the telephone and give her brother a call.

The riches that I believed my estranged uncle possessed were enough of a reason to bring his name up with regularity, but, in time, another presented itself to me. It was the way my mother reacted whenever I raised the subject. She would exhale audibly. Her forehead would crease and her eyes would squint. I relished the sound and sight of such anguish. Using my power to elicit this torture was a great and guilty pleasure.

Gradually, I squeezed some information out of her: Sidney was the third of my grandparents' four children, younger than my mother by two years; growing up, he had been a gifted hockey and football player, and once broke his arm playing the latter; shortly after getting his driver's licence, he accidentally backed over the neighbours' cat on his way out of the driveway, and he wept when he went next door to tell them; he was living somewhere in Montreal now; he had married young but was divorced, and his two children from that marriage, a girl and a boy – older cousins I'd never met – had years ago moved away with their mother to Arizona.

At long last, on a Saturday morning when I was ten, the doorbell interrupted *Jonny Quest.* My mother threw a robe over her holey pajamas and answered the door. Out on the step, unannounced and unexpected, was Sidney. My mother appeared happy to see her brother, but I saw the furrow on her brow.

My uncle's face was tanned. His hair was dark and cropped short like in that old photograph. He was not dressed the way I imagined a man of wealth would be. He wore thick, beige work boots, dark blue work pants, and a matching work jacket that, on the breast, featured an alarm bell logo. He said he had just finished an installation job in the neighbourhood and, seeing as he didn't get up to Montclair very often, thought he'd drop by. He had been surprised when he stopped at our old house on Chapleau Street and discovered we no longer lived there. He found our current address in the telephone book at a payphone, and got our apartment number from the landlord, who'd been mowing his precious lawn outside the complex.

Sidney looked at the couch in the living room, empty now that I had joined him and my mother in the entrance to our place. He glanced in the direction of the opening to our little kitchen. He turned to my mother. "Ralph sleeping?"

My mother's face contorted; she looked irritated and mystified at the same time. She put a hand on my shoulder. "It's going on five years now since Ralph left."

Sidney blinked. His face registered a measure of surprise, but he promptly erased this with a smile. He ruffled my hair with an air of familiarity. He called me Bobby, not Robert, like we were old pals, as if only a few days – and not eight years – had passed since he'd last seen me. He was taller than my mother by a head. They had the same laugh – booming but clipped – and the same small, blue eyes.

"Hey," Sidney said suddenly, his face aglow. He reached into the pocket of his jacket and fished about. I got very excited. I was convinced I was about to get a chance at redemption. Surely my uncle's hand would come out of the pocket holding a bundle of money, bills of different colours. This time I'd know exactly what I was doing.

But it was only a stack of alarm stickers, the kind you put in a window or on a door to warn off burglars. Sidney slipped the top sticker from the stack and presented it to me like it was a Christmas present. Then, with the rest, he turned to my mother. "Let's put a few of these up. Even if you don't have an alarm system, it still gives the idea."

My mother said, "We're renting."

Sidney ignored this statement and, without hesitating, proceeded to place a sticker on the little frosted window in our front door. He went around to the windows in every room of the apartment and did the same. My mother followed him as he did this, a pained, forced smile on her face.

Not ten minutes later, Sidney was gone again.

My mother fished an empty margarine tub out of the garbage can and filled it with hot water from the sink. She took a butter knife out of the utensil drawer. It took her the rest of the morning to remove all of those stickers.

Nearly another decade passed without a word or sign from Sidney. A decade that saw both of my grandparents die; my grandmother first, of a staph infection, speculated to have been contracted at some point after cutting herself on the edge of a can of baked beans she'd opened for my grandfather's lunch; within a year he was gone, too, discovered in his bed, tucked under the covers, appearing no less peaceful than he did when he was sleeping. Morris got into some trouble with government auditors and had to sell his beloved Hewes Bonefisher to pay off the back taxes he owed. And over Thanksgiving weekend in 1988, Kevin's bladder became blocked. He and Christine were separated by then, but it was she who went to pick him up and rushed him to the hospital, my uncle in agony, doubled over in the back seat of her car, unable to squeeze out a single drop. It took emergency surgery to remove the stones.

And while my interest in my absentee uncle Sidney never truly waned, my teen years brought new diversions and pursuits to contend for my attention. Girls, punk rock, parties, and strategies to buy beer at the dépanneur while underage demanded much of my time. But every once in a while, Sidney would still enter my thoughts. Though my encounter with him and his alarm stickers had punched some holes in my beliefs about his money, I still allowed the fantasy of rescue, of a surprise inheritance, and even of a replacement father to play out in my mind. With precious few appearances over the course of so many years, I wondered if Sidney was a recluse, an eccentric, or a combination of the two. Whatever the truth might have been, my uncle was exotic. Knowing he was out there, somewhere, and that I was related to him, made me feel just a little bit remarkable.

I left Montclair when I was nineteen. My mother had been hinting at taking a cheaper but smaller place in the Normandie complex, planning to give up a room of her own for an old sofa bed Kevin was looking to get rid of. I was about to start university, and had already been toying with the idea of moving out. I wasn't going to stay under those circumstances, sleeping in the comfort of a bedroom while my mother spent her nights tossing and turning on a fold-out couch in the living room. I had a student loan and a part-time job at the hot dog and pizza counter at the Club Price in Laval. A new warehouse was opening in Montreal, in Pointe-Saint-Charles. They were looking for employees willing to transfer.

Moving out also meant gaining some needed distance from my mother. She'd always done her best for me, but in my later teen years a kind of sadness came over her. She took up smoking, or, as I later learned, took it up again after having quit for nearly twenty years. She cried in the bathroom a lot. She must have thought I couldn't hear her behind the closed door, beyond her constant flushing of the toilet.

I found a little apartment in Notre-Dame-de-Grâce. It took only a minute to walk from my place up to Sherbrooke Street, where I could catch the 24 bus for the ride downtown to McGill. If a bus didn't come right away, I'd just start walking. Sometimes I walked all the way to school, ignoring the buses that passed along the way. There was so much to see: restaurants, stores, churches, monuments. There were signs and posters pasted to walls and to the sides of mailboxes, announcing concerts, garage sales, lost cats, and free symposiums with titles like *Secrets of the Ancient Druids* and *Unlocking Your ESP Potential.* I felt like I had joined a gripping, much larger world.

One thing that fascinated me on these walks was that I found myself surrounded by hundreds of people – people on foot, on bicycles, in cars and in buses – and yet I was all alone. In Montclair I couldn't make it two blocks down the main street of town before seeing someone I knew. Anonymity was a new feeling for me, and it was surprisingly enjoyable.

I fell into a routine of classes, shifts at the Club Price (where I'd moved up in the world to a position at the Membership counter), reading and studying (not enough), falling asleep after the midnight *Star Trek* rerun on CBC, and, most Thursday nights, going out drinking with a handful of friends from Montclair who had also moved downtown. Near the end of October, I met someone.

It happened in the basement laundry room of my apartment building, where the light was dim and the ceiling was exposed. The room consisted of two washing machines, two dryers, and a rickety wooden chair. She was sitting in the chair the first time I saw her. It was a Friday night; a vague ache still lingered in my head, residue of the pitchers of beer I'd shared the night before at the Cock n' Bull. She was wearing plaid flannel pajama bottoms and a grey, baggy Concordia University sweatshirt. She was reading a paperback. She had dark hair, tied back in a ponytail, and a pretty face that made me feel shy.

She looked up from her book as I entered the room with my garbage bag full of dirty clothes. Our eyes met and we exchanged polite hellos. I found both washing machines in use.

"Mine's almost done," she offered.

"Oh," was all I could think to say.

"Like, two minutes, max," she added. "It's on spin now."

I placed my bag of laundry on the concrete floor and leaned against the wall. I looked at anything but the woman in the chair.

"Have you been living here long?" she asked me.

"A couple of months," I said. "Since September."

"You're a student?"

"I'm at McGill."

"In what?"

"History."

"What are you going to do with that?" she asked. I had fielded this question more than a few times since starting school, but her tone was sunnier than what I was used to, more curious than skeptical. "Are you going to become a history teacher?" She was genuinely enthusiastic.

"That's the plan," I replied, feeling a little gratified. I looked at the cover of her book, Leonard Cohen's *Beautiful Losers*. "And you? You're in English?"

"Commerce."

I glanced at her book again and, despite myself, raised my right eyebrow.

"Oh, this is just for fun." She waved the book a little and closed the cover on a finger, keeping her place. "It's my second time reading it, actually. I'm sort of crazy about Leonard Cohen."

"That's cool," I said, hoping I sounded at least a little cool myself.

One of the washing machines rattled to a noisy stop. My new acquaintance sprang from the chair. With one less machine at work, it was decidedly quieter in the room than it had been before. "I'm Cynthia, by the way," she said.

"Robert," I mumbled in reply. "Bobby. Rob."

A grin appeared on Cynthia's face. There was a measure of warmth and a measure of humour behind that smile. "Pleased to meet you, Robert Bobby Rob."

Over the following weeks, I ran into Cynthia in the laundry room a few more times, and often in the apartment building stairwell. Sometimes, we'd find each other on the same bus heading to or from downtown. Conversations materialized easily, mainly thanks to Cynthia's gentle and genuine inquisitiveness. Her questions made me feel special. It wasn't long before I was beginning each day with the hope that our paths would somehow cross.

By December, with finals upcoming, Cynthia and I were holding nightly marathon study sessions together at her place. We worked side-by-side at her long, simple white Ikea desk. Leonard Cohen watched over us; Cynthia had stuck the *Songs from a Room* album cover to the wall above the desk. I had found it, used, at Cheap Thrills and bought it for her not long after we had shared our first kiss. I should have guessed Cynthia already owned every Leonard Cohen recording, but she seemed touched by the gift. She said a second copy would make an awesome poster.

I never saw anyone work so hard. Unlike me, Cynthia didn't wander over to the window for a peek outside. She didn't lie on the floor and stare at the ceiling. The TV remained off. If I spoke to her, I would inevitably have to repeat myself – she only looked up from her notes when she was ready to. Soon I was inspired to put in a better effort, to try and match Cynthia's diligence, and I forced myself to bear down. She'd poke me with the eraser end of her pencil when I'd fall asleep in my books.

Two-litre bottles of Pepsi and fast food deliveries sustained us. Pizza, mostly, but we ordered souvlaki one night, and poutines on another. One Friday, we decided to call for barbecue chicken.

We placed our order, pooled some money together, and got back to studying. After a while, Cynthia stood up from the desk to go to the bathroom. An idea, a little prank, had been on my mind that night. I saw my chance to put it into action.

Cynthia had this nightgown that she never wore; garishly old fashioned, ankle-length, purple, and decorated with white frills at the shoulders and around an extremely high neckline, it hung permanently on a hook behind her bedroom door. Cynthia thought it was horrid, but she didn't have the heart to get rid of it – it was a gift from her grandmother. It could have easily been a hand-me-down from the same.

I liked to tease Cynthia about it, and I tried to adopt the kind of tone I'd grown up hearing my uncles Morris and Kevin use on their wives. I'd pretend I didn't believe the grandmother story, insisting Cynthia had picked out the nightgown herself, at Zellers. Other times I'd encourage her to wear it, swearing it turned me on just to see it hanging there. "Imagine," I'd say in a lewdly suggestive tone, "if you actually *put it on.*" This usually earned me a punch in the shoulder or chest.

After I heard the bathroom door close down the hall, I quickly stripped down to my underwear. Leaving my clothes in a pile at my feet, I threw the nightgown over my head. I had just enough time to thread my arms into the sleeves before Cynthia exited the bathroom. I pranced my way down the hall, toward her. When she saw me, she put a palm to her forehead. She shook her head and laughed. "You are a total wacko," she beamed.

I was in the middle of an elegant pirouette when the intercom rang.

Cynthia answered, and a man's voice crackled "*Chicken*" through the speaker. Cynthia buzzed the lobby door open and I gathered the money. She put her hand out to take it from me but I walked right past her, down the hall toward the apartment door. "*I'll* get it," I called back, pretending to be insulted by her assumption.

"You wouldn't."

"I would. *You* may be ashamed of the nightgown, but I, for one, refuse to live a lie."

"You are completely insane."

"Hush," I scolded. I was really putting it on. "The only thing insane around here is how crazily comfortable this nightgown is."

It was actually true: it felt light as a bedsheet, more comfortable than I could have possibly imagined. And as I waited by the door for a knock, a broad smile formed on my face. A great feeling of warmth was about my shoulders and neck: the semester was nearly done,

Christmas break was fast on the way, I had an awesome girlfriend (I practically lived with her!), and I was about to freak out a barbecue chicken deliveryman with some ridiculous ladies' sleepwear.

But when I opened the door, it was I who received a jolt.

My uncle, his hair greying now but still cropped short like in that old family photo, stood before me. In one hand, he clutched two cardboard boxes tied together with a string. In the other, a small brown paper bag. He looked me up and down; I saw him raise one eyebrow, briefly, but his face was otherwise expressionless. If my state of dress fazed him at all, he hid it very professionally. "That's going to be twelve sixty-six, please."

"Sidney?"

"Um. Yeah?"

"It's me," I said. "Robert. Bobby."

Sidney cocked his head and stared at me intently. "Bobby? Oh, wow!" He extended one arm as if to shake hands, but the food was in the way. Awkwardly, I took the boxes and the bag from him and pivoted to place them on the floor behind me. When I turned back to my uncle, he was scratching his chin and chuckling quietly. "Jeez, Bobby – does your mother know?"

It was one joke, just six words, but Sidney's delivery was so familiar it gave me a chill. The words were cutting, but the elocution was warm. Dropped into the same situation, either of my two other uncles would have said the exact same thing, in the exact same way.

I found myself, as I'd been doing nearly all my life, attempting to one-up one of my uncles with a joke. "Sure, she knows. She lent this thing to me." As usual, I found my effort wanting.

"Listen," Sidney said, pointing behind him with a thumb, "I've got other orders in the car. It's great to see you, but—"

"Of course," I said. "Here." I held out the money.

Sidney put up a hand. "No, no. It's on me."

"Really? Thanks." There was an uncomfortable pause. On impulse, I filled it. "Hey. We should get together some time."

"Oh, yeah, yeah," Sidney mumbled, backing away. I wasn't sure he meant it, but before turning the corner of the hallway, he said, "Come by the restaurant some time."

I closed the apartment door. I looked at the money in my hand – three blue fives. I figured I was owed at least as much.

Cynthia was standing at the end of the hall.

"What just happened?"

"It's a long story."


I filled Cynthia in on everything. I told her about the different dollar bills and my unfortunate choice when I was too young to know any better. I recounted my childhood assumptions and imaginings about my uncle's wealth. I told her about Sidney's absence from the extended family, about how no one ever talked about him, and about the strange way my mother acted when I brought up his name. Telling these little stories brought me immense pleasure. My heart beat a little faster in my chest and there was a tingly feeling about my ears. That Cynthia was fascinated by the whole affair only added to my fun. And while I was uncertain about what to do next, for her there was no question.

The following Friday, we set out for a late dinner at the chicken restaurant. It was a fifteen-minute walk from our building; I could not help but marvel at how, after so many years spent wondering and guessing about my uncle, I now lived in the same neighbourhood where he worked.

Cynthia and I stomped the snow from our boots in the restaurant entranceway and breathed in the hearty scent of French fries and barbecue. While the place looked clean, its décor appeared to have been last updated in the 1970s. We were greeted by a black pegboard sign on a simple metal pedestal, its white letters arranged to instruct us to wait to be seated. Hanging on a wall nearby was a framed review of the place, yellowed at the edges, clipped from a newspaper dated March 21, 1981. Dark wood strip panelling covered the walls. The floor was speckled black, grey, and murky white.

A waitress arrived to greet us. The burnt orange lipstick she wore almost matched the shade of the dye in her hair. She had a wrinkled face but moved about with vitality. After saying hello, she nimbly pivoted on one foot and, over her shoulder, asked us to follow her to a table. She led us through the dining area to a booth with cushy burgundy vinyl seats. The menu was printed on paper placemats already laid on the table. In the tiled ceiling above our heads, circular patterns of perforations pumped out elevator music.

The waitress left us to peruse our placemat menus. Cynthia stared at me, an expectant look on her face. I knew she wanted me to ask for Sidney, but I was having second thoughts. After years of curiosity, I couldn't help but wonder if I was now invading my uncle's privacy. The waitress returned with two small glasses of water.

"Is Sidney working tonight?" Cynthia asked her.

I felt my face redden.

Cynthia pointed at me. "That's his nephew."

"You don't say." The waitress leaned one hand on our table and stared at me for an uncomfortably long time. "Oh, I see it," she said, finally. "Definitely. I think it's the nose. Does everyone in your family have that nose?"

I couldn't help but place a finger on the end of my nose. "I'm not really sure."

"Sid's out on a delivery now," the waitress said, "but I'll send him over as soon as he gets back."

When we were alone again, I balled up my paper napkin and threw it at Cynthia. "Thanks a whole lot."

She smiled mischievously. "I've always liked your nose."

"I don't doubt it," I answered, feigning annoyance.

"Shut up and enjoy the tunes," she said, glancing up at the ceiling. A soft keyboard rendition of "I Can't Go for That (No Can Do)" by Hall & Oates was playing. Swaying to the beat, Cynthia provided the vocals.

She knew every word.

We were eating when Sidney emerged from the kitchen and approached our table. On her side of the booth, Cynthia scooted over to the wall, making room, offering him a seat. I introduced my uncle to my girlfriend.

"So, was that your nightgown Bobby was wearing the other day?"

"Mine, yes," Cynthia laughed, already charmed, "but I swear, I never wear that thing."

"Of course you don't," Sidney returned, "if he always is."

We chatted for a while, mostly small talk. Sidney had been delivering for the chicken restaurant for about four years; before that he'd had work – he didn't specify what kind – up at Mirabel Airport. I asked him how long he had worked for the alarm company. He looked confused. "Alarm company?" I told him the last time I'd seen him, he'd been installing alarms up in Montclair. "Oh, yeah," Sidney said in a faraway tone. "Not for very long," he offered.

Cynthia, bless her, tried to steer the conversation in a more meaningful direction, but Sidney was evasive.

"So. You're Rob's mother's brother?"

"Yeah, but *he* can tell you that."

A man in a gravy-stained apron appeared in the kitchen doorway and waved at Sidney.

"Gotta go. Delivery time."

Just then Cynthia began to hop up and down in her seat, a look of pure joy on her face. Sidney, who had slid out of the booth, stared at her, intrigued. I wondered what could have been causing her to act so delighted, so suddenly. When our eyes met, she pointed at the ceiling. Then she began to sing. *Suzanne takes you down to her place near the river.*

Sidney turned to me, puzzled.

"She's crazy for Leonard Cohen."

"Really?" Sidney angled an ear toward the ceiling. Then he brightened. "I deliver to Leonard Cohen sometimes, you know."

"Come on," Cynthia said.

"Yeah, yeah. It's true. He calls once or twice a week. He gets the Half-Chicken Dinner. With extra sauce."

A picture appeared in my head: Leonard Cohen sitting on a couch, a paper napkin tucked into his collar like a bib, stooped over a takeout box of chicken on a coffee table, greasy fingers dipping French fries into one of two Styrofoam containers of barbecue sauce. It seemed utterly ridiculous.

"Oh my God," Cynthia said. "That's *unbelievable.*"

"You really like Leonard Cohen?" Sidney asked, sounding skeptical.

"Like him? I *love* him. There's no one better."

An expression of great seriousness came over Sidney's face. For a moment he stood still and silent. He appeared to be considering something of great importance. Finally, he sat back down in the booth and leaned over the table, drawing our heads nearer to his. He turned and peeked over his shoulder in the direction of the kitchen. Then he turned back to us. In a hushed tone, he said to Cynthia, "You should come with me, the next time Cohen calls. You can bring him his order." Then, looking only at me, he winked.

"Are you crazy?" Cynthia said. "I'd be so nervous I'd barf."

"Okay," Sidney sang. "I mean, if you don't want to meet him—"

"I'll do it!" Cynthia said. Then she grabbed my hands across the table. "But you have to come with me."

"I wouldn't miss it."


When I told my mother I had made contact with Sidney, she responded with silence.

"Hello?" I said into the telephone receiver.

"Hello," she replied, monotone.

"Is something wrong?"

"What do you want to go and get involved with *him* for?"

Now it was my turn to be silent; I didn't know what to say.

"What right does he have to even *talk* to you?"

"I don't know, maybe because of the fact that we're *related?*"

"Related," she spat. "Big deal. Everything was fine the way it was. You don't need him in your life. You didn't need to go and find him."

"Mom. I didn't go on some big quest to find him. It's like I told you: I ordered chicken, he delivered it."

"So stop ordering chicken."

"I really don't get it, Mom. What is your problem with Sidney?"

"*My* problem?" She sounded enraged. "Who says *I* have a problem?"

"Okay, okay," I said. "I'm not saying you have a problem. It's only a figure of speech. What is *the* problem? What is *the* problem with Sidney?"

She didn't answer me right away. I waited for her. "He's a strange bird," she said. Quickly, she added, "And that's all there is to it. Are you coming up this weekend?"

Her attempt to change the subject was a cue, and I let the matter go. My appetite for provoking my mother was not as strong as it had once been.

When I hung up, I noticed that the fingers of my left hand, the hand that I hadn't been holding the phone with, were clamped across the middle of my palm. I relaxed my grip. Four short lines, indentations, marked the spots where my fingernails had been digging into my skin.

Sidney's call came two weeks later. Cynthia's excitement was palpable. We jogged up to Sherbrooke Street, slipping on the slick sidewalk, laughing. In the cold air, our breath came out like steam. It was the same colour as the pale grey sky overhead. When Sidney pulled up in his car, I let Cynthia get in the front seat. I crawled into the back, next to a stack of takeout meals. The interior of my uncle's car had the same warm and succulent barbecue scent to it that the restaurant did; the tree-shaped air freshener hanging from his rear-view mirror was superfluous. Sidney did a U-turn in the middle of the intersection and we headed west.

Cynthia didn't think to put her seatbelt on until we were stopped at a red light.

We parked in front of an apartment building on Sherbrooke near the corner of Walkley. After we all got out of the car, Sidney handed me two fives and a ten, plus a handful of coins, to make change with. He also passed me a brown paper bag filled with utensils, napkins, and a container of coleslaw. Then, holding the cardboard box by the string that was wrapped around it, he presented Leonard Cohen's Half-Chicken Dinner to Cynthia. She took it with both palms upturned, beneath the box. She winced – it was hot to the touch.

Sidney made a clicking sound with his tongue. "Here." He pinched the string with his fingers again and lifted the box from Cynthia's hands. "You're supposed to hold it by the string."

"Good to know," Cynthia said, with humour in her voice. She cleared her throat. Her cheeks were flushed and she blinked a few times in rapid succession. She took the box back in the prescribed manner, dangling it away from her body.

"Find his name on the board and call him on the intercom," Sidney instructed. Cynthia nodded and turned toward the building. I followed her, and when I passed my uncle our eyes met. He gave me a wink.

Of course I could have stopped it all right then.

But I was feeling too important; there was a glow about me that I was enjoying too much, the satisfaction of being in cahoots with one of my uncles was too enchanting.

I could say that I didn't know what was going to happen (or – perhaps more believably – that it was only in that very moment, with that particular wink, that I began to wonder if something was up), but that would be a lie. Because I knew. Of course I knew. My uncle's wink outside the apartment building was merely confirmation of what I'd known, deep down, all along. Because this is what men in my family do. With a chuckle that sounds warm, and with a knowing, well-timed (and well-aimed) wink, we tease, belittle, and trivialize the women in our lives. This was our entertainment. *They* were our entertainment.

The directory on the wall in the lobby of the building had two columns of names inside tiny rectangular windows. There was a little round button beside each name. Halfway down the first column, we found *Leonard Cohen*, written, like all of the other names, in scraggly cursive on sun-bleached paper. Cynthia bit her bottom lip and rang Leonard Cohen's bell.

The intercom clicked. Barely above a whisper, a man's voice purred, "Yes?" Maybe in that moment Cynthia pictured Leonard Cohen's face; maybe she imagined that his eyes were only half open and that his lips were but a centimetre from the microphone on his end.

She took a step back, her eyes wide, and stared at the intercom. I looked at her and cocked my head toward the speaker, urging her to say something. She shook her head, terrified. The voice came through the speaker again, now sounding irritated. "Hello?"

"Um," I began. "Chicken?"

Cynthia and I climbed two flights of stairs and made our way down a brown-carpeted hallway with white stuccoed walls. An apartment door at the end of the hall opened at the same time that we arrived in front of it.

A grizzled old man stood in the doorway with a fistful of five-dollar bills. He wore a billowing yellow cardigan, unbuttoned, atop a pea-green polo shirt. His plaid pants, two shades of brown, were held up by a belt with a Donald Duck buckle. His wispy white hair was longish on the top and brushed precariously across his scalp, turning up slightly at the ends. It looked like the slightest draft would have dislodged it. The old man waved his money with one hand and gestured at the food with the other.

He was a terrible tipper.

When the apartment door closed again, my heart was still racing from the thrill of the prank, of the betrayal. There was a sort of ecstasy, too – ecstasy laced with just the slightest inkling of nausea. I smiled expectantly at Cynthia, the way you smile at someone right after they've opened your Christmas present. She was scowling, her face bright red. "Your uncle is a total jackass."

"Well," I laughed, "that was Leonard Cohen. That was a Leonard Cohen."

Her expression changed from anger to one of disbelief. "Did you know?"

I hesitated to answer. I tried to contain the smile Cynthia's question had prompted. I tried to dull the twinkle it must have brought to my eye.

She stormed past me, twisting her torso so that her back was flush with the wall in the hallway. No part of her body touched mine.

I jogged after her down the hall and down the stairs, calling her name, but Cynthia wouldn't stop, wouldn't look back. She punched the door to the lobby open, and did the same to the door to the outside.

Sidney was waiting for us down on the sidewalk, arms crossed, leaning his back against the passenger side of his car. With a big satisfied smile on his face, he watched Cynthia approach his position. When she marched right by him, he called out to her back. "Hey, how about if next week you help me deliver to Pierre Trudeau? He lives on Benny Crescent and he gets the Double Leg Special!" Cynthia stopped at the tail end of Sidney's car. She swivelled, and pounded the trunk with the base of her fist. Sidney ducked, feigning shock, and curled both of his forearms over his head, as if an explosion had gone off beside him.

Cynthia took no notice of this. She was already walking swiftly away from us.

Sidney straightened. Steam billowed from his mouth and nostrils as he chuckled to himself. He looked at me and, again, winked. His gesture expressed warmth for me, but somehow it didn't feel like it was coming from a familial connection, from the fondness of an uncle for a nephew. The feeling of connection that I was getting from Sidney came from a different place altogether. It came from both of us being men.

I had one foot pointed toward Cynthia, who was growing smaller and smaller in my vision, and the other pointed toward my uncle, the man I had so many questions for, the man I had desperately wanted in my life for as long as I could remember.

"Not the sharpest tool in the shed, is she?"

"Pardon?" A cold sensation washed over my chest.

"Her. What's her name – Cindy? She fell for that one easily enough, didn't she?"

"Um. I think I better—" I pointed in Cynthia's direction.

"Yeah, you better. You better or you'll be sleeping on the couch for who knows how long. What're you gonna do, eh? Girls."

All I could bring myself to do was look at my uncle and shrug.


Cynthia had much to say to me. When I opened my mouth to speak, she shut me up before I could utter a word. She said she would tell me when it would be time for me to talk. I thought, *Fair enough.*


I never told my mother about the Leonard Cohen stunt. And she never asked me about Sidney again. It was easier that way, I think, for both of us.


In the spring, I found myself passing by Sidney's restaurant. I had no intention of stopping, but the waitress who had served Cynthia and me back in December was in the big window of the place, wiping the glass. She waved me inside.

"Could have sworn you were Sid when I saw you coming down the street. A sight for sore eyes that would have been, eh?" She laughed.

I tried to process the waitress's words.

"Where's he gone, anyway?" she asked with genuine curiosity and a hint of concern. "He didn't tell anyone when he quit."

I didn't know what to say. I considered inventing something – a new job, maybe a new town – just to keep up appearances. I considered admitting my ignorance, appearances be damned.

I dithered long enough to provide the waitress with an answer.

"He didn't tell you, either," she marvelled. She shook her head and let out a little laugh. "What a guy."

The news that my uncle had moved on from the restaurant did not surprise me. A part of me, on a level barely detectable, had expected it. The only thing I felt about this development was relief. My uncle Sidney was absent, his whereabouts were unknown, and the date of his next appearance – if there ever was to be one – was uncertain. This was the man I had always known.

Before leaving the restaurant, I ordered a family-size French fry to go. I took it back to the apartment to share with Cynthia. She'd be home soon.

# STINKY UP A TREE

## I

Jane is pulling lunch from the oven when she is struck, and momentarily stunned, by the realization that an unhappy milestone has arrived: Lorne has been down on the living room floor for exactly four weeks now.

She pauses, trance-like, bent before the open oven door, waves of heat on her bare arms and face, supporting a baking sheet in one oven-mitt-swathed hand. Four weeks have passed – an entire month, without the smallest hint of improvement – since that Saturday afternoon when Lorne began to grumble about a pain in his leg. Since first complaining his leg was *on fire*.

The edges of the baking sheet are blackened from use; the familiar pattern of burn marks releases Jane from her torpor. She knocks the oven door closed, sets the baking sheet down on the stovetop, and removes the oven mitt from her hand. An open-face tuna melt steams before her, melted orange cheese still sizzling from the broiler. Jane uses a spatula to transfer it from the baking sheet to a ready cutting board. She slices into it with a bread knife and crisp baguette crumbs fly up like sparks, strewing onto the melamine countertop. An undetected glob of hot cheese oozes onto Jane's thumb and she winces at the burn. She thrusts the edge of her thumb between her lips and dabs at it with her tongue. With more caution, she makes a second cut, and the tuna melt is divided in three: two generous pieces, equal in size, and a third, smaller serving.

Jane has already prepared handfuls of tomato wedges and cucumber sticks on Lorne's plate, and she slides one of the larger portions of tuna melt alongside them. She sprinkles salt and cracks pepper over the tomatoes and cucumbers. She tugs the jangling utensil drawer open, plucks out a fork, and bumps the drawer closed with her hip. With the plate in one hand, she snatches a can of ginger ale from the refrigerator and marches from the kitchen.

In the adjoining living room, Jane deposits the plate and the can onto the hardwood floor at the head of the mattress. Lorne is lying on his back, his head cradled on one of the good pillows from their bedroom.

"Do you want a glass?" Jane asks.

Lorne turns himself over, slowly, methodically, his face crumpled in pain, until he is lying on his stomach. Both cheeks puff out and he exhales long and audibly. He reaches for the ginger ale can and pops open the lid. "No glass. Thanks."

Jane turns on her heel and returns to the kitchen.


The sciatic nerve, the doctor in Emergency had explained, is the longest in the body. "It begins in the lower back," she'd said, folding one arm behind her own back, "and runs all the way down both legs, to the feet and toes."

Jane, back to the wall, wedged between a stainless steel sink and the foot of the examining table on which Lorne lay, listened quietly to the doctor's prognosis. She hadn't anticipated being allowed to stay in the room, but after she'd delivered Lorne there, supporting a good portion of his weight on one of her shoulders, the doctor closed the door while she was still inside. Lorne made straight for the table, eager to lie down and relieve the pressure produced by being on his feet, and the doctor went right to her work. Jane took it upon herself to silently occupy the small open space by the sink.

The doctor told Lorne the problem surely originated in his spine, most likely a herniated disc, and that disc was compressing the sciatic nerve, explaining why he felt the pain down his leg.

"So, I need surgery?"

"No surgery," the doctor replied with a patient smile on her face. "It might take a while, but sciatica will clear up in time, without having to resort to surgery."

"But the pain," Lorne said, pitifully.

"I'll write you up something for that."

The examination was over but Lorne remained prone; lying horizontal upon something firm was the only position that offered him any, albeit scant, relief. Watching the doctor with her prescription pad, Jane began to feel some relief of her own. She knew it was excruciating for Lorne: she'd never seen him cry from pain before, only for hockey games and, if he didn't hide it well enough, Rodgers and Hammerstein musicals. If medication could spare him some of the agony, Jane would be spared some of the sounds of his suffering.

The doctor handed over the prescription and Lorne began the arduous task of standing again. Jane emerged from her spot between the sink and the examining table to lend a hand. The doctor offered her a sympathetic smile. Then, turning to Lorne, she asked if he had any idea how he'd injured himself. His answer came swiftly. "Painting."

Jane flinched, but recovered herself, smoothing back her bangs with her fingers.

"I was standing on a chair, I guess I was lazy, and I stretched to get a spot."

"Did you fall?" the doctor asked.

"No. I just stretched. Too far. I should have just gotten down and moved the damned chair."

"You never know with these things," the doctor said. "One false move—"

About a week before the visit to Emergency, Lorne had finally started painting Jesse's room. It needed – Jesse needed – an update. It seemed like their son had turned sixteen overnight, but deep down Jane knew baby blue had run its course long ago. She had been bugging Lorne to do the job for a year. The cans of plain white paint she'd bought had sat stacked in the hallway for so long that they'd become as much a part of the surroundings as the dusty baseboards, the linen closet door, and the old school photographs of Jesse that lined the wall.

Jesse had been only too happy to bunk on the couch in the basement, with unfettered access to the television down there. And Jane had been happy to see the work progress, feeling the tension the languishing project had been causing her begin to dissipate. And then, in bed, on the night before the first signs of his pain set in, Lorne had asked Jane, again, to do *that thing*.

So many times, in so many different ways, she'd refused; by pretending to believe he was joking, by pretending not to hear, by pretending to be excited by something else. This time, however, she'd yielded. Why this time, she could not pinpoint. The thought that the requests might stop if she'd grant him this one crossed her mind. She could also admit, barely, and only to herself, to feeling a tug of obligation, a vague notion that Lorne's painting should be rewarded. And then there was the thought that she'd done it out of a sense of what she could only call duty, though not to him, that she was sure of. But if not to him, then to who? Or to what?

Whatever the reasoning, concede she did and now, the story went, it was the act of painting that had put him on the floor. Painting, and not the arrangement of parts, better suited for a pair of circus contortionists, that had him inflamed but to her seemed ridiculous; some awkwardness to tolerate, get over with, and move forward from, hopefully never to be asked for again. Painting: the thing *she* had asked for. And a reminder of it every time a doctor, a relative, or a friend asked how the sciatica had set in. A reminder of it for four weeks running, every time she saw him lying on that crummy fold-out mattress on the living room floor, watching television or reading or snoring, his scraggly beard growing longer by the day, his hair frowzy like a tramp's.

Jane places the smaller piece of tuna melt, cooler now, on her own plate, next to her own tomato wedges and cucumber sticks. She returns the last, larger, section of tuna melt to the oven, to keep warm for Jesse. She picks up her plate, but before returning to the living room, goes to the back screen door and prods it open with her foot. She calls for Stinky.

The cat was out all night and, now a little past noon, Jane hasn't seen her all day. A few kisses in the air usually brings her bounding from wherever she happens to be hiding or prowling, to the kitchen, purring, with a firm but tender bump of her furry head against Jane's shin. Today, however, none of Jane's attempts have produced any results. She shudders, wondering if this is it, that time when, by means of a car, a dog, or some other tragic fate (the owl scenario she's concocted really gives her the chills), the cat just doesn't come home anymore.

Jane joins Lorne in the living room. She begins to eat her lunch on the couch with her plate on her lap, a sheet of paper towel balled in one hand. She stares at the television. An old movie she doesn't recognize, though she does recognize Steve McQueen.

"This is delicious," Lorne mumbles from his mattress at her feet. He gives the tip of his thumb a quick suck, and then does the same to his forefinger. He dabs at the crumbs on his plate. "Isn't Jesse coming for lunch?"

"He's supposed to."

"He's late again."

"Sixteen-year-olds are late a lot."

"He should be more responsible."

"How's the pain?" Jane asks, attempting to steer the subject elsewhere.

"Creeping up on me."

"When can you take your pills?"

"At two."

Jane takes a bite of her tuna melt, the cheese squeaky between her teeth. She looks at Lorne. He has a stack of paperbacks down on the floor, beside his head. The radio that normally sits on the kitchen counter is down there, too, next to the books, the cord trailing under the couch to the outlet behind it. The television is always on. Jane marvels that a person can live like this - immobile, on a floor - if he has some meagre means of entertainment. Lorne sleeps more than the cat does now. The cat. "Have you seen the cat today?"

"I saw her out the window."

"When were you at the window?"

"I wasn't. I saw her going up." Lorne rolls over on the mattress, carefully, his face contorting with pain, until he is lying on his back. He points at the big bay window. Then he flicks his finger upward. "I saw her going up the tree."

Jane puts her plate aside and springs to her feet. She goes to the window and looks outside. The grass around the big oak is littered with acorn shells. The squirrels have been busy gorging themselves for a week now. She places her hands on the window sill and cocks her head sideways, peering up. The oak's trunk is thick and knotty. The branches start a good fifteen feet up from the ground. The tree itself, by her best guess, is fifty feet tall, maybe closer to sixty. She scans the branches, the dense green, and, with a shiver, she spots the cat.

Stinky is three-quarters of the way to the top of the tree, perched on a branch, her mostly black fur standing out against the surrounding leaves. "Oh my God," Jane says. "She's way up there."

"Way up?"

"Way, way up."

Jane jogs to the front door and goes out onto the front porch. Now that she's closer to the tree, Stinky's roost seems even more precarious than it had appeared to be from the window. Jane walks toward the tree, bare feet on grass, calling the cat by name in a soft and high-pitched voice. She kisses the air a few times in quick succession. Stinky's ears perk up. She bends her head slightly to one side. But she makes no other movement. Instead, she meows. A plaintive and sad meow, Jane thinks. She squints up at Stinky. She balls both of her hands into fists and places them on her hips. She calls the cat again. Stinky replies with another meow. Jane places a palm on the trunk of the tree, rough and dry. She walks the perimeter of the tree and blinks up at the cat again. A cramp materializes in the base of her stomach, fear manifested as discomfort. She returns to the house.

Jane walks straight down the hallway toward the kitchen, passing the living room without looking at Lorne.

"Did she come down?" he calls.

Jane opens the pantry door and grabs the box of Meow Mix.

"So," Lorne calls again, "did she?"

"No," Jane mumbles as she walks past the living room again. Out on the front porch, she shakes the cat food box and calls Stinky. This captures the cat's attention, but still there's no indication of movement.

Lorne is yelling something at Jane. She stops shaking the cat food box to listen. "Try pouring the food into a bowl. To make that plinkity-plink-plink-plink sound."

Jane looks down at her bare feet. All of her toes are curled. She is also squeezing them. She inhales deeply and relaxes her toes. Lorne's idea is worth a try. She returns to the house.

"Did you hear me?"

"I'm getting a bowl right now."

Back outside, Jane places one of their soup bowls on the porch. She bends, and shakes cat food from the Meow Mix box into the bowl. She steals a glance up at Stinky. The cat meows. Jane calls to her. Lorne is yelling from inside the house again.

"Pour it back in the box and pour it into the bowl again. Make that plinkity-plink-plink-plink sound again."

*Fuck you and your plinkity-plink-plink-plink sound.* But Jane tries his idea. She tries it three times before she gives up and goes back inside.

"I'm going to call Serge," she announces.

"I'm sure he doesn't work on Saturdays," Lorne says.

"He'd come. For the cat."

"Do we have to call Serge for every little thing?"

"Stinky up a tree is not a *little thing.*"

"But what can Serge do about it?"

"He has a big ladder," Jane says.

"I'm sure he has lots of big equipment."

The blood rises in Jane's face. Roughly, she grabs up Lorne's lunch plate, and then her own. She marches from the room, stomping her feet, ignoring Lorne's singsong claim that he was only joking.

She plunks the lunch plates into the sink with a clang and runs the hot water right on top of her unfinished tuna melt. She despises those jokes. The suggestive ones. The ones that imply intimacy. She knows – God, she certainly hopes – Lorne doesn't really think there's anything between her and Serge, but his little jokes encourage the imagination. And this despite Serge's age; over a quarter-century her senior, in his

late sixties, and though he's a very *young* late sixties he is in his late sixties nonetheless. Imagination induces guilt; guilt for noticing things
like his height, well over six feet, the generous width of his hands and
the length of his fingers, and even his nose, which is large, but *propor-
tionally* so. She is reminded of the old game she played at sleepovers as
a child, when one girl would say to the others, "Don't think about
butts," causing torrents of laughter as everyone, for the next few minutes, thought of nothing but. It is tortuous to feel remorse for a thing
that has never happened but that now exists, vividly, in her mind. She
pushes the soggy food to one corner of the sink and rinses the plates
longer than necessary, allowing the hot water to redden the backs of
her hands.

The hot water had turned cold one day some three years ago. Lorne
had dutifully felt the water for himself, holding his hand beneath the
faucet for a full minute before affirming that, indeed, it would not
become hot. He examined the faucet carefully, as if some outward clue
to the source of the problem might present itself. He turned the water
on and off, predictably to no effect. The sudden flash of an idea brightened his expression and, with eyes wide and one finger held in the air,
he marched to the bathroom, where he checked the faucet there. It,
too, ran cold, even when he turned the hot water tap on all the way,
splashing the counter and the front of his shirt.

It was Lorne's mother who gave Jane the name and number of a
man from her Horizon Club bowling team. Recently retired, good
at odd jobs, lots of time on his hands. She watched from the window
that first time Serge arrived in his army-green pickup truck with a silver box cover over the cargo bed. An extension ladder poked out
from the box's open back window, a red handkerchief tied to the top
rung. He parked on the street in front of her and Lorne's cars in the

driveway. He exited the truck with a cigarette dangling from the corner of his mouth. He took a few steps toward the house, stopped, and smoked his cigarette down. He threw the butt away in the street and started again for the front door.

Serge entered with a pleasant smile and an unhurried gait. He didn't ask for permission to leave his shoes on in the house; he simply strode straight into the kitchen. He ran the water, felt it with his fingers, and asked if anyone had checked the pilot light.

"Pilot light?" Lorne had said, as if hearing an unfamiliar, foreign term. Then he reddened. Jane saw him bite his bottom lip. She thought he probably wished he could just disappear. And, filled with equal measures of love and pity, she had wished he could, too.

Jane hears footsteps behind her and she shuts the water off. She turns from the sink. Lorne is on his feet, in the kitchen doorway, grimacing. "I'm sorry." He is still wearing yesterday's sweatpants and undershirt. Jane feels a little guilty and a little disgusted.

"You shouldn't stand if it hurts."

"I know. But I want to say I'm sorry."

"Why don't you take your pills early?"

"Maybe I will."

"I'm going to call Serge."

"I know."

Jane shakes two little white tablets from Lorne's prescription bottle and pours him a glass of water. "Here," she says. Lorne pops both pills into his mouth and follows with the water. "Now go back and lie down," Jane says. She nudges him a little and he turns, shuffling cautiously, in the direction of the living room.

Jane makes her way to the corner of the kitchen counter where they keep the telephone book. She flips it open and thumbs through pages without reading them, her eyes on the doorway. When Lorne finally disappears from view, Jane closes the telephone book with a thump. She goes to the telephone on the wall and picks up the receiver.

Savouring the tickly thrill of it, she dials Serge's number from memory.

## II

A decade prior, Lorne had been dead set against naming the cat Stinky. It was a ludicrous thing to call a pet. He'd thought of his father – an oft-employed measuring stick – and imagined him in the same situation: arrive home from work to find that his wife and six-year-old child have adopted a stray cat that they've seen fit to name *Stinky*. The cat itself, Lorne's father *might* have tolerated. But never the name. Lorne told Jane that no respectable family had a cat named Stinky.

Jane stifled a laugh. "How many respectable families do you know?" She poured white wine into a glass for him, her own drained and in need of refilling.

There was a part of Lorne that wanted to laugh, too. To be in on the joke. He even liked the cat's looks: completely black but for a thin loop of white on its chest and little white patches on each of its four feet. But he hadn't been consulted; a decision had been made before he even got home. Something was compelling him to put his own stamp on the matter.

He switched his focus from Jane to Jesse. He sternly told his young son a new name would have to be found for the cat. When the boy asked why, Lorne stated, borrowing his father's commanding cadence and what he imagined his firm words would be, "Because Stinky is *not* a name."

Jesse ran from the room, crying, "But it's *her* name!"

"Did you have to make him cry? Was it *that* important?" Jane topped up her glass and drank a swallow. "Don't you wonder why he named the cat Stinky? Does any part of you even want to know?"

Lorne's feelings were divided. He was angry, impatient, and, at the same time, racked with guilt. With a wave of his hand, he prompted Jane to explain.

"Look," she began, "that cat showed up this morning, lying around on the back deck. But every time I'd go outside, it would run off. And after I'd go back inside, it would come back. And then, when Jesse got home from school and saw it out there, he went tearing outside and the cat – I'm telling you – the cat didn't budge. She was completely calm. Jesse was down on all fours, right in her face, and she didn't even flinch. In fact, she rubbed him with her head! That thing loves him. And he loves her."

"I imagine he fed her something? That's called *hunger*, not love."

"No, no. This was way before we gave her anything to eat. Jesse came in for his snack, and the cat followed him right into the kitchen. Of course, Jesse was just ecstatic. And then, it was the weirdest thing: Jesse asked me what the cat's name was. I hadn't even thought about that, but seeing she's so black, I said '*Inky*.' Then Jesse started to laugh and he sat down on the kitchen floor and the cat was rubbing its head against his legs, and Jesse said, '*Stinky's purring! Listen! Stinky's purring!*' So I corrected him, told him the name I was thinking of was *Inky*. Then, and this is the strange part, and I promise you it's true, Jesse looked at me like he was totally disappointed in me, like I had just said two plus two is five. The cat was walking circles around him and then Jesse said, '*Come here, Stinky.*' And that cat curled right up in Jesse's lap. It was just so weird."

Jane's story put Lorne in a mood. There had been other occasions when he'd felt a little gloomy after hearing anecdotes from her day with

Jesse: a funny thing the boy had said, an adorable reaction to a situation, or some other charming episode that had occurred while Lorne was at work. He had always attributed his downward swings to regret; something he considered perfectly normal to feel - but not express - for being absent from memorable moments. He was not the only father around who was experiencing them second-hand.

But this story about a cat and how it came to get its name was different. The melancholy was there, present and familiar, but so was another feeling. An unexpected feeling and one that was, for Lorne, troubling. He attempted to deny it in his own mind, to push it away, but the truth was, he was jealous. He resented having to be away; he was bitter about the things that went on without him. He didn't want to feel this way, and he told himself to snap out of it. But Lorne could not stop coming back to the scene he'd formed in his head, the scene based on Jane's description of the afternoon, and he could not stop wishing *he* was the little boy down on the kitchen floor.

Playing with his new cat, his mommy's feet reassuringly nearby.


Down on his mattress, Lorne feels the first hints of his medication at work. Spindly fingers of numbness begin to blunt the pain in his leg, and to muddy his head. It's a sensation he welcomes - sleep will soon follow, but first he'll be stoned for a little while.

He can hear Jane in the kitchen, speaking on the telephone. She'll bring Serge into this. Serge and his truck and his tools and his abilities. His know-how and his skills. Serge, whose mere presence reminds Lorne of the things he doesn't know how to do. Who makes him look stupid in front of his wife and his son.

Jesse's been veering out of control. Apathetic about his school work, coming home late, probably drinking and who knows what else. He's getting away with too much. Lorne had let him get away with naming the cat Stinky. If only he'd put his foot down then, things might be different now. If he didn't expend so much energy trying to keep Jesse in line, maybe he would have time to read a how-to book, or to take a class at night or on weekends, and maybe he'd know how to fix things on his own. Maybe he'd be the one wielding the screwdriver in this house, maybe he'd be the one hammering the nails. And maybe, if he hadn't let things slide, he'd be the one climbing a ladder to rescue the cat.

He doesn't even own a ladder.

Lorne smiles and chuckles quietly, irritation giving way to giddiness, teetering on the edge of opiate slumber.

His eyelids droop and Lorne conjures the scene once more, from ten years ago, when Jane told him the story of how Stinky got her name. He recalls how Jane had looked at him expectantly, trusting he was about to laugh or maybe even squeeze her hand. Instead, he'd stifled sentiment and the loosening effects of a second glass of wine to declare, coldly, that if Jane and the child wanted to call the cat Stinky, *they* could do so. He, on the other hand, would not be using that name.

"What will you call it, then?"

"I won't be calling it at all."

That's what his father would have said. Lorne knew then and he knows now that he'd nailed it.


## III


École Secondaire Sainte Sylvette is a red-brick, two-storey building. The schoolyard, surfaced in concrete, is found in the back. Six picnic tables sit toward the rear of the yard, lined up in two rows of three, their wooden benches and tabletops faded to a pallid grey. Beyond the tables, an eight-foot cedar hedgerow separates the school's property from the neighbouring retirement home, blocking the view of both establishments from either side of the bushes.

Pushing up through cracks in the concrete throughout the schoolyard are small patches of sturdy, stubborn weeds. The space where the yard meets the school's back wall is particularly lush. A staircase of a dozen concrete steps juts out from the wall, leading up to the school's back entrance. One side of the staircase is closed off by a triangular wall of cinder blocks. The other side is open, making the dark, cave-like space beneath the stairs accessible not only to the school's janitor, but also to generations of seclusion-seeking Montclair teenagers.

Jesse is hiding out in the cool, shadowy crawl space beneath the stairs. He's stoned, and his stomach is full of raw Pillsbury cookie dough. He sits on the cracked concrete ground, his back leaning against the wall behind him, his arms resting loosely on his drawn-up knees.

He's been smoking up with Darryl and Stuart. Darryl has been Jesse's friend since kindergarten, when the two used to share a seat on the school bus and amuse each other to the point of hysteria, whispering swear words back and forth, real ones and concocted ones. *Shampimple*, never formally defined, more valuable for the way it sounded than what it might have actually represented to either of them, was a co-creation the two still recall and occasionally – especially when stoned – utter to mutual delight.

Stuart is a newer friend, whose orbit Jesse and Darryl have been progressively entering since the end of Grade Ten, when his reputation for an ability to acquire pot and hash began to solidify. While Stuart shares Jesse's passion for the Montreal Expos and after-school *Welcome Back, Kotter* reruns, Jesse appreciates and quietly prizes the extraordinarily convenient aspects of their friendship. As long as Stuart is around, there is no need for Jesse to own any of his own stuff; no risk of ever being caught with rolling papers, matches, lighters, lighter fluid, tweezers, clips, cigarettes, pipes, or the drugs themselves.

In the dark, smoky chamber beneath the stairs, Jesse passes the cylinder of cookie dough to Darryl, who is sitting right next to him. He watches Darryl bite into the thick stick. He observes that his friend chews with mouth open and askew, like a cow. Jesse turns away, sickened by the sight of partially masticated dough between smacking lips.

Jesse knows Stuart, though out of sight, is not far away: from somewhere out in the schoolyard, his voice can be heard clearly. It is, actually, Elmer Fudd's voice, or at least a decent impersonation of Elmer Fudd. "Shhhhhh. Be vewy vewy quiet, I'm hunting wabbits." It is, when stoned, Stuart's thing.

Stuart appears in the opening of the exposed side of the stairs. He has a large stack of cedar branches, some green, some dead and brown, cradled in his arms. He dumps his load at the edge of the entrance. Jesse snickers at this mysterious, ridiculous course of action. "What the fuck are you doing?" he calls out jubilantly.

"Shhhhhh," is Stuart's reply as he walks away, again out of sight. "Don't scare de wabbits."

Darryl cracks up hysterically. His head flops against Jesse's shoulder. Jesse leans away from him, also laughing. He tries to push Darryl off of him, but he is a dead, stoned weight. The two jostle clumsily and giggle stupidly until Stuart returns with another heap of branches. Feigning authority, Jesse declares, "You're damaging this school's property."

"Shhhhhh," Stuart whispers in Elmer Fudd's voice, "I'm gonna smoke doze wabbits out." He drops the new branches on top of the others and walks away again.

"You're a fucking nutcase," Jesse calls out. He reaches for the communal pack of du Mauriers and slips a cigarette from the box. Turning to Darryl, he asks, "Where's the light?"

Darryl paws around his general vicinity while staring straight ahead, dreamily.

"Stuart!" Jesse yells. "You got the lighter? Stu!"

Stuart returns to the edge of the crawl space without answering. He adds yet more cedar branches to his collection. The loose pile now reaches the highest part of the opening, blocking out some of the meagre light that had been making its way in before.

"Stu," Jesse says, a little impatient, "pass the lighter."

"Wabbits don't need wightas."

At first, the dripping sounds, coupled with the little puddle that begins to form beneath the branches, makes Jesse think Stuart is pissing. "You fucking pig," Jesse laughs.

He stops laughing when the scent of lighter fluid hits him.

He hears the repeating click of Stuart's Zippo. The whoosh of ignition sounds quickly and powerfully in his ears. The branches are all aflame.

"Oh, shit!" Darryl yelps, scrambling to his haunches.

"Oh, shit!" Stuart repeats, in his real voice, from the other side of the fire.

Jesse crawls a few inches toward the crackling blaze, but intense heat sends him scurrying back. "Stuart!" he screams. "Stuart, put it out!"

"I'm trying!" Stuart shouts back. "It's too fucking hot!"

"You fucking idiot!"

"I said I'm trying!"

Grey smoke billows and thickens, quickly filling up the small space beneath the stairs. Jesse's heart races in his chest. Fruitlessly, he scrambles for an alternate escape route. Darryl crawls further away from the fire, all the way to the cinder-block wall. He whacks at it with an open palm, shrieking wildly, an expression of terror on his face. Jesse holds the collar of his T-shirt over his nose and mouth, but the smoke still chokes him. He coughs. He is seized by the chilling notion that he is living his last moments.

With utter clarity, Jesse decides to not die in such idiotic fashion.

He crawls to the cinder blocks, where Darryl is still screaming for help. Jesse stands as close as possible to the back wall, where the slanted ceiling beneath the stairs is tallest, where he only has to slouch slightly to be upright. He clenches his fists and runs as fast as he can at the flames. At the last second, he closes his eyes and mouth tightly, and dives at the burning branches. He crashes through the fire and rolls onto the cement of the schoolyard, skinning his elbows and knees, bumping his left shoulder. But he is out of danger.

Adrenaline pumping, Jesse picks himself up off the ground and darts back to the mouth of the fire. Stuart looks on with wide and astonished eyes, his mouth and nose covered with the sleeve of his jean jacket. Jesse kicks wildly at the branches, but the heat is too intense to keep up the effort for very long. Darryl is still screaming on the other side. Stuart, meanwhile, is backing away from the scene, looking shaken, pulling his jacket collar to his nose.

Jesse runs at him.

"Dude, dude! I'm sorry! I'm so sorry!" Stuart raises an arm in front of his face, bracing for an assault.

Jesse grabs Stuart by the shoulders of his jean jacket. He pulls at it. "Take it off," he shouts. "Take it off now, you fucking idiot!"

Jesse returns to the fire. He whacks at it with the jean jacket, pounding it out in some places, scattering burning branches in others. "Darryl! Get out! Get out!" Darryl scrambles safely from the crawl space, hacking.

Jesse begins to kick at the remaining burning branches, driving them away from the building, dividing them into smaller clusters. He glances at Stuart, who appears dumfounded, standing stock-still with hands clasped together atop his head. "You could help, you know."

"Seriously," Stuart says, joining Jesse, "I'm really sorry. It was just a joke."

Jesse no longer feels the effects of the pot he's smoked. The three boys go about trampling out the remains of the fire. When the job is done, Jesse asks if anyone knows the time.

"Ten after one," Darryl answers, looking at his watch.

"I'm fucked," Jesse says.

"What's wrong?"

"My dad. He's being a dick about meals and I'm late already. I'm out of here."

He walks away from his friends and briskly crosses the schoolyard. When Jesse reaches the corner of the school's back and side walls, he hears Stuart shout out his name.

"Don't let him spank you or anything!"

"Yeah," Jesse calls back. "I'd like to see him try."

Jesse makes his way along the side of the school and, when he reaches the sidewalk out front, turns in the direction of home. The sky is choked with clouds. A flock of seagulls soars high overhead. The outline of each individual bird stands out clearly, almost brightly, against the pale canopy of grey. And Jesse finds himself unable to resist hoping his father *will* try something. Again.


The first time his father tried something was during spring break. It was a Friday night and Jesse had been late – a good three hours late – coming home from a party. But he had a reason for being late; an excuse so infallible, so noble even, that Jesse was actually eager to reveal it to his parents.

Jesse's enthusiasm transformed into dread when, approaching the house, he found the porch light turned off. Every window in the house was dark, too. A subtle message was never clearer to Jesse. No warm, welcoming glow would be offered to a scoundrel as disobedient as he; no electricity would be wasted on this offender.

He felt little surprise to find the front door locked. All of his friends had their own keys to their houses, but Jesse, according to his father, had not yet earned enough trust to merit one. He was forced to knock.

The door swung open instantaneously; his father had been waiting. He slapped at the light switch in the vestibule with his palm. Jesse felt like a convict lit up by a spotlight, caught attempting escape from the prison yard. All he wanted to do was sulk back to his cell.

Jesse stepped into the vestibule but found he was blocked to advance any further. His father stood, hands on his hips, in the doorway that led to the living room. Annoyance shaped his brow, screwing up his eyes. Jesse peered past him and saw his mother sitting on the couch, arms folded, also irritated. He looked at his father again.

"Just where do you get off coming home at this hour?"

Jesse snickered. "*Get off*," he mimicked.

"What's that?" His father took a quick, hostile step toward Jesse. His mother stood up from her seat on the couch.

"I'm not *getting off* anywhere," Jesse complained. "I'm late, yes, but did you ever think to ask *why*? Did you ever think I might actually have a reason?"

Abruptly, without warning, Jesse bolted forward and squeezed between his father and the vestibule doorjamb. He stomped down the hallway toward his bedroom.

"Jesse!" his mother called.

"Don't talk to him, Jane," his father commanded. And, with dramatic flair, he added, "You can't talk to a drunk."

Jesse stopped short in the doorway to his bedroom. He flung his head back. He opened his mouth wide, squeezed his eyes shut, and laughed. He laughed rowdily, like it was the funniest thing he'd ever heard. *You can't talk to a drunk* was such a ridiculous exaggeration to Jesse that open mockery came as a reflex. The longer he laughed, the more his laughter felt like a weapon. And he aimed to administer pain.

From behind, both of Jesse's arms were seized up around the shoulders. He stopped laughing. He was tugged at roughly, his father attempting to spin him around to face him. Jesse widened his stance and planted his feet firmly on the floor, keeping his face forward, refusing to physically comply. He stared into his bedroom, where Stinky reclined amid the unmade blankets on his bed, observing the scene with feline indifference. He felt his father yanking at his arms again, but resisting the pull was unexpectedly easy. Jesse felt a wave of warmth flow through his body: it was pride. Pride in the discovery of his own strength, and pride that his father was discovering it, too. He felt he could stand there all night, immovable.

His mother sounded frightened, calling his father's name first and then Jesse's. Her hands entered the fray, and attempted to loosen his father's grip. And then, without it ever feeling like a conscious decision, Jesse stopped struggling. He let his body go slack.

In an instant his father had him turned around. They were nearly eye-to-eye, Jesse barely an inch shorter. His father was red in the face, infuriated. Jesse only smiled. And then he was pushed. Pushed into his room with some amount of force, but – again, unexpectedly – less than he'd imagined his father could muster.

Normal momentum would have carried Jesse two or three steps, but now it was his turn to exaggerate. Like a professional wrestler inside the ring, Jesse propelled himself further, all the way to his bed, and, once close enough, flung himself at it. He was airborne for only a second, two at the most, but it was long enough for Stinky to dart from the bed. Jesse flopped to the mattress, rebounded slightly, and lay there.

He played dead. He felt giddy, and pleased with himself. His only regret was the fright he had given his cat.

Jesse is not far from home now. With every house he passes, he thinks of the people who live inside them, people he doesn't know, and who don't know him. People who will hear, over the coming days, about a mysterious fire at the school. They'll gossip and complain, speculate and guess, but they will never know who did it. Or that someone jumped through the fire to save himself.

He'll have to enjoy that knowledge privately.

His house in view, he can see Serge's truck is parked in front of their driveway. He is relieved: Serge's presence will temper his parents' reaction to his being late. But he can't help but feel some amount of disappointment as well. Stirred from rehashing the spring break incident, a part of him had been looking forward to yet another confrontation.

His mother and Serge are in the front yard. Walking up the driveway, Jesse spots a tall silver ladder leaning against the big oak tree. Serge has one foot on the first rung and one foot on the ground, staring up into the tree. He's also eating something, taking a bite of what looks like baguette. His mother stands beside Serge, also peering up. Jesse follows their lead and cranes his neck to see what has them so mesmerized.

"It's the cat, Jesse" his mother says. "She's way up."

Jesse searches the tree branches. He spots Stinky, higher up than he expected her to be, higher than he's ever seen her climb.

"I'll give it another try," Serge announces. The handyman stuffs what's left in his hand into his mouth – Jesse can see now it's his mother's tuna melt – and jostles the ladder's front rails, checking its stability against the trunk of the tree.

"You don't have to go back up," Jesse's mother says with compassion, laying a hand on one of Serge's big forearms. "Really. It's too high. You could hurt yourself." She glances at Jesse and then quickly looks away, withdrawing her hand.

Jesse thinks he might laugh, he thinks he might gag. He resists the urge to do either. Unconsciously, he turns his head toward the house. He spots his father in the bay window – only his head is visible – watching the proceedings from one of its lower corners. Their eyes meet, and his father's head bobs down and out of view.

Serge has moved away from the ladder. Jesse has a clear path. He marches to it and, in one fluid motion, begins to climb. Ascending, he hears his mother calling him down. She sounds frightened, just the way she sounded on the night of the big fight. Jesse takes each rung faster.

He'd never told his parents why he'd been late, and they'd never asked. He'd never described the scene at the party; the toppled furniture, the broken glasses and beer bottles, the splashes and stains on the walls, the ripped patio screen, and, in the kitchen, amid the empties, cigarette butts, and garbage, the grains of rice – the entire contents of a bulk bag – strewn all over the floor and the counters. The party had gotten out of hand and order was only restored when Sharon Ladd went beet red in the face and began to sob. She was distraught: her parents had explicitly forbidden parties while they were away, and now the house was inundated with evidence of a wild one.

An exodus began almost immediately, kids scattering out the front door, Stuart – Jesse's ride – included. It would have been so easy to just run like the rest of them, especially with Stuart urging him to bail with him. But Jesse couldn't bring himself to abandon the scene. A sense of duty had come over him, aided, perhaps, by the beer and the pot his head was swimming in, but something about Sharon's hysterics had struck a chord. There'd be no parties at all if people like her never took the risk to have one. Jesse decided to stay and help clean up.

"What are you, a janitor?" was all Stuart said before disappearing out the front door.

In addition to Jesse, a half-dozen others came back, and they all got to work. Sharon, recovered somewhat, thanked them ceaselessly throughout the cleanup. "And especially you, Jesse," she'd said during a particularly exuberant demonstration of gratitude when the job was nearly done. "You're the only boy who stayed."

Jesse blushed at the compliment and tried to appear nonchalant. Inside, however, he glowed with elation.

Jesse is so high up the ladder he doesn't dare look down. He has loved this cat for a decade, since a time that seems so long ago now, but never before has he felt such devotion. To anyone.

After he'd fallen asleep the night of the big fight, he'd been awoken by scratching at his closed bedroom door. He'd gotten out of bed and opened the door. Stinky slinked in, rubbing against his ankle as she passed. She slept at the end of his bed that night, between Jesse's feet, like so many nights before, purring loudly. Before falling back asleep, Jesse had felt like turning from his back to his side, but he didn't. So as not to disturb the cat.

Jesse finally arrives at Stinky's branch. He stretches out his arm but the cat is just out of reach, sitting on its haunches, staring at him intently. Jesse calls her by name and kisses the air. Stinky cocks her head. Jesse calls her again. This time she rises, and takes one tentative step toward Jesse. Her pace suddenly quickens, walking the branch, her claws stabbing the wood with every step. Jesse draws his arm back toward his body. Stinky reaches his shoulder and bumps it with her head.

"Okay, now," Jesse says in a gentle tone, "come with me now."

Gently, he hooks his arm beneath the cat's belly. She arches her back, raising her underside, making herself slippery. Jesse swiftly lifts his arm to match the cat's evasive manoeuvre, and hoists her up and over to his chest. He cradles her there, firmly.

"Oh!" His mother's voice below is squeaky. "Be careful!"

"He's fine," he hears Serge say.

Jesse, with only one hand free to clutch the rungs of the ladder, descends slowly and methodically. Stinky purrs deeply against him, her fur tickling his chin. Jesse speaks to her softly the whole way down.

When he reaches the ground, his mother places her hands on his shoulders and squeezes them. The cat squirms to be free, and Jesse lets her pour from his arms. "That was incredible!" his mother cries.

"That cat really trusts you," Serge chuckles, pulling a cigarette from his pack.

Jesse looks at the living room window. His father is back down in the corner again. Slowly, solemnly, he makes a fist and raises one approving thumb.

"You must be starved," his mother says. "Why don't you go in and make yourself some toast." She turns away from him, adding, "I'll help Serge put his things away."

Jesse mounts the porch, Stinky at his heels, and opens the front door. He feels giddy, much like he did the night of the fight: surprised by – and proud of – his own strength, his own abilities. He steps inside the house, but stops in the vestibule: an unanticipated thought has formed in his head. He stares at the floor beneath him, and at his feet. For the first time, he understands that a day will come when those feet will carry him across this same threshold, but in the opposite direction, for good.

# LITTLE BROTHER,
# REMEMBER THE CHRISTMAS?

## Wookiee Brown

Remember the Christmas when you got into Mom's purse? They caught you in the closet, lipsticks and keys and coins and tissues on the floor, encircling you like a wreath. You were building a little pyramid of pills, your fingers chalky with pink dust.

"What did you eat?" the nurse at the hospital demanded to know.

You didn't answer.

"What did it taste like?"

I was sitting next to you on the examining table because I'd screamed until they'd let me. We were drawing on the crinkly white paper beneath us with one crayon each. I'd convinced you to take the stubby brown one ("Whoa. This is *Wookiee* brown.") and took the newer-looking red one for myself.

"What did it taste like?"

You looked up from your picture and said *Pepperoni* like it was a question and Dad giggled, clamping a hand over his mouth.

The nurse exhaled audibly. "How many did you eat?"

One hesitant hand holding up four fingers. Then five. Then two. Then one finger up your nose, excavating. Dad cracked up. "This is no laughing matter," the nurse scolded. "This child could die."

"Hark! The Herald Angels Sing" was playing in the corridor when they dragged us out of there by our hands. I pointed at the speaker in the ceiling, a perfect circle of perforated dots, but you weren't listening.

Remember you fell in the parking lot and ripped the knee of your snow pants? That's when they noticed you didn't have your mitts but Mom said I'm not going back in there.

You sure loved pepperoni. I ate that red crayon on the ride home.

## The Grouch and Jonas Grumby

Remember the Christmas when your present was an Oscar the Grouch finger puppet and mine was a Skipper from *Gilligan's Island* action figures? We filled a big bowl with Rice Krispies, called it quicksand, and made them sink in it. The arm of the couch was a cliff and we made them fall off. It was an inspired idea, you had, to make the toilet tank Oscar and Skipper's secret sewer hideout, but I dropped the top of the tank on the floor, it was a lot heavier than I thought it was going to be, and it broke into two pieces and that was that for *that* Christmas.

## Halves

Remember the Christmas when we moved? It was minus-twenty and we ran out of boxes and Mom pulled out the kitchen drawers and we carried them one by one to the car and dumped their contents into the trunk. Remember your feet got so cold that Mom sat you on the edge of the tub with your feet soaking in hot water? She told me to stay with you and good thing, too, because you fainted, fell backwards, and I caught you. You woke up and you were screaming and your nose was running and Mom gave you a Children's Aspirin and we got in the car and drove. Mom looked small behind the wheel but then she moved the seat up. I thought she was going to take you to the hospital again but we went to McDonald's. The manager was wearing a pointy green elf hat with a bell on top that jingled as he walked back and forth behind the counter. We had cheeseburgers and glasses of water. You and I got extra because Mom split her cheeseburger in half and then split one of her halves in half. She placed those two smaller pieces on our flattened, yellow cheeseburger wrappers. My extra had the pickle in it.

## Mint Extractions

Remember the Christmas we spent at Roger's? He gave us each a slim box of peppermint patties. Like miniature hockey pucks with bumpy chocolate tops and smooth chocolate bottoms. White goo inside that made our breath feel cold. You hated the mint but you liked the chocolate. You had only one of your two front teeth and you were so meticulous, biting the top off a patty. You scooped out the mint with a sweep of one finger and then you ate the bottom. You did that with your whole box, *The Sound of Music* on the black and white TV in Roger's basement, and you wiped the mint extractions on the walls. On the drive home Mom said you'd deserved that slap but she hadn't and that's why she was mad at you.

## G.I. Joe and Frozen Dead Tauntauns

Remember the Christmas when Dad came back? He had grown a beard and shaved his head to stubble. Mom laughed and rubbed his scalp and called him G.I. Joe. He had two blue Krazy Karpet sleds in one arm, a paper bag of groceries in the other. We marched down the hall, dragging our sleds, following Dad's snowy boot-prints to the kitchen where he said *ta-da!* and from the grocery bag produced a lobster. It was suspended in water inside a transparent plastic bag that looked about to burst. Brown and alive, slow-motion antennae probing and seeking, it had pink rubber bands wrapped around its claws. You cried when Dad told you the lobster wasn't a pet and you locked yourself in the bathroom when you found out it was for dinner. You came out when they promised not to eat it, and they sent us outside with our sleds to wait for Dad to take us to the hill. We walked around and around the house, our legs sinking into the snow past our thighs, pretending we were stranded on Hoth and our tauntauns were frozen dead. We kept our eyes to the sky for signs of a rescuing snowspeeder.

We rang the doorbell to ask when were we going to the hill, and they kept saying soon, and after a while they just stopped answering the door. When the sun was gone, we decided to try the snowbank out front. The ride down was short and bumpy but the road was icy enough for us to make it all the way into the driveway across the street. The neighbour stormed outside and escorted us back home and rang the doorbell and we told him they're not going to answer that but he banged on the door until they did.

"Do you have any clue what your kids are doing? In the dark?"

Dad, his lips greasy, a plaid tea towel tucked into his V-neck like a bib, said, "Do you have any clue what I'm going to do to you if you don't get out of my sight?"

You saw it first, clutched in Dad's hand, the lobster's red claw, the rubber band gone, and you ran, wailing, and we drove around looking for you forever. We finally found you in the playground behind our school, sitting at the top of the slide that, because of the snow, was half its usual height. The front of your scarf was stiff with frozen saliva. They said you were definitely on the naughty list.

The next morning Dad was gone again but he'd left the Krazy Karpets behind.

## Répondez, S'il Vous Plaît

The dépanneur across the street from my building sells boxes of Rosebuds. They're smaller than peppermint patties but they don't have any mint goo inside.

I'm thinking about putting them in a bowl.

So, if you're not doing anything, could you – would you – come over for Christmas?

# THE BORDERLAND

"Ron has CH."

"Ron has C-what?"

"C-H."

"I have no idea what that means." I plucked a frying pan from the rack beside the sink and dried it with my dish towel. We were cleaning up before bed – something I hadn't felt like doing but something, Amy had made clear, that came with a reward. And it wasn't even a trying night.

"Chronic halitosis. Ron has chronic halitosis. You didn't notice?"

I laughed. I hadn't heard that terminology in a long time. "Well, yeah. I noticed. But his breath always reeks."

"But it's really bad now. It's like vinegar. My eyes were practically watering."

A close-up image of Ron's goatee-encircled mouth appeared in my head and I shuddered. His chapped lips.

"He's really starting to give me the creeps."

"Starting to?"

"More than usual." Amy handed me a wet spatula. "He's saying things he shouldn't say, he's talking about things he shouldn't talk about. To people. Like that broomball stick story. So gross. He really needs a girlfriend."

"Yeah, well, I mean – would you date him? Would you even consider it?"

"Are you crazy?"

"Would you send a friend out on a blind date with him?"

"Never."

"Then you see the problem here."

Both of Amy's hands were submerged in suds, scrubbing the cake pan that she'd made brownies in. She'd packed up the leftover brownies and presented them to Ron when he was leaving. "Don't forget your Ronny bag." He'd have made it back to town by then, back to his apartment, not far from where Amy and I used to live. Knowing Ron for as long as I had, there wasn't a doubt in my mind that he was, at that very moment, sitting on his couch and polishing the brownies off. A movie would be playing on his TV, something like *The Towering Inferno* or *Caddyshack*, and there'd be a week's worth of dirty dishes piled in his sink and no one to nag or bribe him to wash them.

I looked at Amy's slender calves, the little furrows behind her knees, a glimpse of thigh. Black skirt and a sleeveless silver top. I focused on the side of her neck, the little mole that she called a freckle. I wanted to kiss it.

"Why don't you just let that pan soak?"

"We're getting it all over with tonight."

I stepped in behind Amy and slowly reached around her. I skimmed a dollop of soap suds off the surface of the sink water and cupped it in my palm. It crackled quietly. Amy watched my hand, a dry smile on her face.

"Don't even try it."

"Who, me?"

Amy pulled the cake pan from the water and pivoted to face me, the dripping pan a shield. I took one step back as her eyes met mine. She smiled and her face was flush. I faked with my head, then faked with my suds. She shifted the pan around to match my moves. She was laughing.

"Are you cold?"

"No." She trembled slightly.

I motioned with my chin at her upper arms. "Because you've got goosebumps."

She looked down and to one side to study an arm and I moved in with my handful of suds. She let out a short, pointed shriek and quickly, abruptly, hauled the cake pan up higher and smacked my fingertips with it.

"Oh! Lukas! I'm sorry!"

I shook my hand out and the suds stuck to my pants and to the floor. I laid my bad fingers in the palm of my good hand. It hurt like hell but I could tell it wasn't going to last long. "Jesus. You're dangerous."

"Is it bad?"

I looked at her and smiled. "I wouldn't be surprised if I end up losing two, maybe three, fingers."

Amy feigned annoyance and deposited the cake pan in the dish rack. She reached into the sink water and pulled out the stopper. "If you're too hurt, if you're suffering, I'd understand."

"I think I might be okay."

"I thought you might be."


I took it upon myself to raise the subject of breath with Ron. We were having lunch in our truck, in a Costco parking lot, a slab of pizza in its box on the dashboard. "Maybe a doctor would have some ideas," I offered. Ron just looked at me and chewed. His Transitions lenses were shaded. He had an irritating habit of folding his pizza slices in half, allowing him to eat faster and, as a result, consume more than me. "It's just that people are starting to notice," I continued. And, because I felt bad, added, "I think."

Ron sipped Sprite through his straw. Condensation from the bottom of his plastic cup dripped onto his wrinkled beige shorts. He crammed the remains of a pizza slice into his mouth and reached for another one. He folded the tip back to the centre of the crust, holding it in place there with his thumb.

"It's not a race, you know."

For a moment, the only sound in the truck was that of Ron's chewing. Then he lifted his thumb. Slowly, the pizza slice unfolded itself, gradually coming to rest in its original shape, drooping toward his lap.

Amy and I were in the IGA. I told her it was a bad idea to not invite Ron to the dinner she was planning. I was holding a transparent produce bag open, she was filling it with half-ripe avocados. "He'll find out, somehow. Plus, he really likes Mexican food."

She said she needed a break from Ron. From his breath. His stories, his comments. "And anyway, do really think he'll want to come up to Montclair again so soon? He certainly teased us enough about it. *You might as well have moved to Chibougamau.*"

"Ron and I tease each other all the time."

"Fine. But do you think he's going to want to hang around with us if we have a baby?"

"Why wouldn't he?"

"Do you think we're going to want him hanging around?"

"Why wouldn't we?"

Amy stared at me. I couldn't tell if the expression on her face was exasperation or pity. Maybe it was both.

There'd always been some amount of talk between Amy and me about having kids, but I had managed, for what seemed like forever, to stall her. I'd bring up finances, I'd mention emotional readiness – anything to talk her down. I wasn't completely against the idea of becoming a parent, it was just that Amy had one very specific - and very firm - stance on the matter: we were not raising children in the city.

She had her mind set on the suburbs, a place like where she'd grown up. "Somewhere with parks and bike paths." I pointed out that Benny Park was not two blocks from our apartment, and that there was hardly a shortage of bike paths in Montreal. She looked at me like I had suggested we'd be sending our future children out to play in Sherbrooke Street traffic.

I didn't want anything to do with the suburbs and their cookie-cutter houses, their lifeless strip malls, and their grocery store bagels. I pointed to couples we knew who were making a go of it in the city with kids, but Amy would not be swayed. She wanted a yard, she wanted flowers, she wanted trees. She wanted her own childhood.

As frightening as these conversations were for me, I had time on my side. As long as we weren't actually trying to have a baby, as long as we were still saving up, still preparing, the whole business seemed to be far off in the future. And that distance was comforting.

But then, out of nowhere, it just happened. By accident, without trying, without me ever giving in. Amy was pregnant. I was scared, but Amy got busy. She called the doctor, bought a stack of expecting books and drew up a budget. She got us a real estate agent. We spent our weekends driving out to places like the West Island, Brossard, and Chomedy to visit houses for sale.

Amy's enthusiasm and command of the situation took a lot of the worry off of my mind. I even made her a card, sort of. I cut out letters from newspaper headlines and ads and concocted a ransom note, taped it to our bedroom door.

I HAVE YOUR BABY. CONTINUE BEING THE MOST AMAZING PERSON ON THE FACE OF THE EARTH AND I'LL LET YOU HAVE HIM OR HER (I'M NOT TELLING) IN ABOUT 9 MONTHS.

SINCERELY,
YOUR WOMB.

She loved it. Got tears in her eyes and everything.

The day we first visited the townhouse in Montclair, I nearly talked Amy out of going in the first place. I was tired and didn't feel like spending another Sunday out in the boondocks. "Isn't living attached to other people supposed to be one of the reasons to leave the city?" She thought about this for a while. And she'd been throwing up that morning. She considered taking a nap. But then she said, "Oh, let's just go see it."

I was polite during the tour of the place but I was only going through the motions. The interior looked serviceable, with three small bedrooms, a living room no bigger than the one in our apartment, a decent kitchen, and an unfinished basement. Finally, we were taken out to the back yard through a patio door in the kitchen.

It felt like I was in the final scene of *Miracle on 34th Street,* when Susan and Doris and Fred stumble upon the house that Kris Kringle slyly leads them to. Like young Susan in the movie, Amy was enraptured. The yard itself was small, with a little flower garden and a box vegetable garden. But the door in the back fence opened directly onto a park. Her eyes wide, a big smile on her face, Amy paced the park, and put her hand on a slide, a jungle gym, a swing set, and a metal rocking horse. There was green grass and there were birches, maples, and firs. There was a path that led, the real estate agent informed us, to another park. Amy applauded.

We submitted an offer that night and celebrated by opening a bottle of Chilean red for me and a carton of Tropicana for Amy.

Ten days later, at breakfast, with the sale finalized and just over a month before we took possession of the house, Amy and I were sitting across our kitchen table from each other. She wasn't eating. She just stared at her Mini-Wheats.

"You awake?" I asked.

"I don't feel pregnant."

"What are you talking about?"

"What I said. I don't feel pregnant anymore." She looked terrified.

We both called in sick and I drove her to Emergency. She cried the whole way. I kept asking her if it hurt, was she in pain.

"No!" she snapped. "I told you, I feel nothing!"

It took all day but they finally got us into an ultrasound room. Amy lay down on the table and I stood beside her. We held hands. The technician went to work while the doctor watched the monitor, which showed us granular, black and white images that looked like the surface of the moon, out of focus. How anyone could tell what we were looking at, what we were supposed to be looking for, was beyond me. Nonetheless.

Amy wept and I squeezed her hand. I stroked her hair. The doctor was nice and called Amy honey and told her it wasn't her fault, that it just wasn't meant to be, that things just hadn't worked, this time. That it happened to lots of women, including the doctor herself. That in a few months, Amy could try again. Then she looked at me and said "Sorry."

I bit my bottom lip. I couldn't stop wondering if there was some way to parlay this development into cancelling our move to the suburbs.

I was feeling nervous on my way to work on the Friday before the party. Amy had made me promise not to tell Ron. Just this once. But now I was facing a full day with him in the truck, and he was bound to ask about the weekend. He always did. And when I saw our delivery sheet had only three stops on it, I got even more anxious. It would be a slow day, with plenty of time for chatting.

We started at an apartment building in Notre-Dame-de-Grâce with a queen mattress and box spring, too big for the old elevator. We hauled them up three flights of stairs and then barely got them through the apartment door. The place smelled like frying meat and the lady was frantic, insisting she was supposed to get a free DVD player with her order. Dressed in a lemon-yellow bathrobe, she hurled insults at Ron and me as if we had personally sold her the deal in the showroom. Ron called it in and dispatch told him to tell her it was being looked into. It wasn't good enough. She kept yelling. Ron said he'd go check the truck again, though we both knew full well there was no DVD player in there. It was just his personal, if temporary, escape plan. I wished I'd thought of it first.

In the apartment doorway, with the lady's back turned to him, Ron bobbed his head at me and pantomimed smoking. I patted my breast pocket, letting him know the pack was on me and not in the truck. He flashed me a pleading look.

I winked back.

Ron disappeared into the hallway. I pretended to listen to our client's ongoing complaints for another minute. Then, as if I'd suddenly thought of something, I reached into my pants pocket. I pulled out my keys and jangled them, making a big show of it. "My partner," I said, shaking my head. "He forgot the keys to the truck. I'll be right back." The lady kept on talking, I heard her all the way down the hall.

I decided to take the elevator. It was one of the oldest ones I'd ever seen on the job. I was confused by the fact that the beige elevator door had a doorknob on it. It also had a small, diamond-shaped window at eye-level. I stared through it into the darkness of the elevator shaft, could make out two dangling cables, barely. I pulled on the door handle. It budged maybe half an inch but remained closed, safely locked. I pressed the single black button, no Up or Down. Some rattling issued from behind the door. The elevator's arrival was signalled by a change in the window: darkness became beige, the same beige as the door. It was a second door, an inside door, which subsequently slid open, and the window lit up with the light of the elevator car's interior. I tried the doorknob again. This time the door yielded to my pull. It was heavy.

I rode down to the lobby. There was a bumpy landing. The inside elevator door opened, revealing another closed door like the one upstairs, with another diamond-shaped window. I peeked through it before exiting. The front entrance of the building was right in front of me, two glass doors. Beyond them our truck, outside, parked abreast a fire hydrant. No sign of Ron. I pressed my forehead against the window and peered to the left. He was there, near a corner of the lobby, his back and palms pressed against the wall, sucking his stomach in, head turned to one side, toward the door to the stairwell next to him. He was expecting me to come through that door, from the stairs. He was waiting to scare me. To earn points in an ongoing scaring competition we'd lost score of long ago.

I kicked the elevator door open and, simultaneously, in my best authority-figure voice, shouted, "*Excusez-moi, monsieur! Qu'est-ce que vous faites là?*" Ron yelped and grabbed at his flabby chest. I started laughing. He put both hands on his knees, head down. He breathed and laughed. He stood up straight again. His glasses were shaded just a little in the indirect sunlight of the lobby.

"Motherfucker."

"You brought that upon yourself. You left yourself wide open."

"There's gonna to be payback." He was panting. "There's going to be a big payback."

"I'm shaking."

Ron whooped and made for the front door. "Let's go smoke," he said. I followed. He turned suddenly on his heels and lunged at me. "Boo!" I caught a whiff of his garbage breath and raised a hand in front of my face. Ron looked happy with himself, adjusted his crotch. "That wasn't it."

"That wasn't what?"

"The payback."

"Obviously."

We went outside and Ron's phone rang. I handed him a cigarette while he talked and lit one up for myself. Passed him the light. His glasses went completely shaded. When Ron hung up, he told me dispatch said the lady was right. She'd bought the mattress during a promotion that finished two months ago, but had put off delivery until today. We were to inform her her DVD player would be sent over that afternoon by taxi and to expect a ten-percent discount cheque by mail, for the oversight. There were only two stops left on our delivery sheet for the day, including one on Lakeshore Road out in Pointe-Claire, which meant a drive by the water. Lunch could be stretched out.

"So, we're having this dinner thing tomorrow night. No big deal, but stop by if you want. Quesadillas."

"Sweet. What time?" Ron took a haul of his cigarette. He spiralled smoke out his nostrils. I didn't answer him right away and he looked at me. "What?"

"You really have to do something about your breath. Amy's having people from her office. People talk. People judge."

"Don't worry about it. I'll get it under control. Promise."


Amy and I tried again that Friday night. Fourth night in a row. She had a little calendar on the table next to her side of the bed, blocks of dates with Xs. Most of the Xs were highlighted. It was a little mechanical but I wasn't complaining. Amy highlighted another X and we went to sleep.

The next morning I woke up first and started making salsa right away. Chopped onions and garlic, seeded jalapeño. When Amy walked into the kitchen, she looked sleepy and annoyed. I mentioned there was coffee ready. She said her eyes were stinging and why did I have to make the salsa so early in the morning. "Sorry. I'll open a window." I was trying to get a jump on the preparations, to take some of the stress away. To make it easier to tell her, eventually, that Ron was coming. The moment had obviously not yet arrived. I volunteered to switch to cleaning and left the cooking to her, waiting for her mood to change.

I was in the living room, bringing drinks to some of Amy's work friends, when the doorbell rang. Amy came out of the kitchen and walked into the front entrance area, but before she could open the door, Ron's voice blared from the other side of it, identifying himself as the police. Amy didn't laugh. She just unlocked the door and left it open on a crack, turning back toward the kitchen. On her way there, she gave me a dirty look. I was a little bit drunk and I smiled, wide, made a sweet face. She squeezed her nostrils between her thumb and forefinger and disappeared into the kitchen.

A little tentatively, Ron let himself in. He wiped his feet on the doormat. He was wearing his beige shorts and a black T-shirt with a picture of Yoda on it. His Transitions lenses were still tinted from the outside. And he had a yellow surgical mask strapped over his mouth and nose. I marched over.

"Hey," he greeted me, his voice slightly muffled.

"What the hell are you doing?"

Ron looked at me. Though eyes were shaded and his mouth was covered, I could tell the expression he wore on his face was perplexed.

"Is this supposed to be a joke?"

"I tried gum," he said, quietly. "I tried Scope. A whole bottle practically. It got a bit better but it didn't last. The mask does the trick, though. I'll just say I'm getting over the flu. That I'm being considerate."

Amy was in the kitchen doorway behind me, leaning on it, arms crossed. Silent. Her eyes on me.

"I'll cough once in a while," Ron offered. "To make it seem real."

"Look, dude. I think you better just leave."

On Monday, Ron called in sick. A guy from the warehouse, Anthony, replaced him. We were on the road two minutes and he asked me if I'd mind if he smoked. "Be my guest," I said. He promptly lit up a doobie. "Jesus! Put that thing out. You're going to get us both fired!"

"Sorry, man. It's just so great to get out on the road. You and Ron have it good, man. You have it real good."

Anthony had much to say, held many opinions, which he shared with me from the passenger seat, happily and unprompted. He jumped from issue to issue. Nuke the North Koreans before they nuke us. Legalize pot and prostitution. Jail the file-sharers. And on and on.

Mid-morning we found ourselves not far from Ron's apartment. I told Anthony I wanted to stop by for a minute to check on him. He could smoke his joint in the alley if he wanted. He thought it was a great idea. "Hey," he said, "give Ron a message from me. Tell him don't get well soon, okay?" He laughed, pleased with himself. "A joke. Just a joke. Shit, this is fucking great, the road."

The scent of cigarette smoke and burnt toast greeted me as Ron opened the door to his apartment. He was wearing a checkered robe, two different shades of grey. Black socks and bare, white calves. "What do you want?" His glasses were tinted just a little. I realized they were always tinted, at least just a little.

"You ever think of getting new glasses?"

"If you've come here to criticize me again, go away."

"Sorry. I didn't mean it that way. I was actually trying to be helpful but never mind."

"Fuck off." He turned and walked toward his living room. I followed him. His place was tiny.

"Look, I'm sorry. For the other day. I shouldn't have thrown you out like that. It's just that Amy—" I was distracted by Ron's TV. Pedro Martinez on the mound, in an Expos uniform, on pause. "Which is this?"

"The brawl."

"Cincinnati."

"Yeah." Ron had an impressive collection of Expos games on tape.

"Put it on for a minute," I urged. I sat down on Ron's prickly beige couch. "We were there."

Ron plopped onto the couch, too, and clutched the remote. He pressed PLAY. "VIP section for the first three innings."

"And the usherettes would have never noticed us if you hadn't insisted on going for hot dogs," I chided. "I told you you'd get caught on the way back into the VIPs."

"I seem to recall somebody asking me to bring him back a beer?"

"You were going anyway!"

"For the record, it wasn't hot dogs that I went for," Ron said with mock haughtiness. "It was a milkshake."

I laughed and then Ron did, too. I turned my attention to the TV screen. "Look at how skinny Pedro was."

"He was young."

"He was perfect for what, six innings?"

"Seven and a third."

"Until he hit—"

"Sanders."

"Reggie Sanders."

"What an idiot."

"As if Pedro would bean somebody on purpose in the eighth when he's five outs from throwing a perfect game."

"Total idiot, Sanders."

It had been a long time since I'd talked about baseball and it felt good. Evidently, Ron and I had not forgotten how. I watched Martinez hurl a fastball past Roberto Kelly for a called strike. Dormant thought patterns were coming back to life in my head. The video was grainy, old. "You still watch your tapes a lot?"

"Usually while I eat," Ron said. "An inning or two. Sometimes just the eighth and ninth. Depending."

"I haven't watched nine straight innings of baseball since they took the Expos away." Not-so dormant bitterness was stirring.

"This is the only baseball I watch. I can't watch actual, live baseball."

"Fuckers." We watched a couple of outs in silence. I couldn't take it anymore. "This is too sad."

Ron pressed STOP on his remote. The TV feed took over the screen. *The View.*

"Whoa, that's sadder."

Ron laughed and turned the TV off. "I gotta piss." He shuffled from the room.

A mirror hung on the wall above Ron's TV. It was narrow and oval and framed in cheap black plastic. It was covered in dust. I'd been with him the day he pulled it from somebody's garbage, around the same time as the ball game we'd just been watching. He'd never upgraded, never needed to. Or was it he'd never wanted to? A cheap wall mirror, a shitty apartment, a surgical mask at a dinner party. These things simplified Ron's life. They freed him to watch VHS tapes of fifteen-year-old baseball games while eating fish sticks with ketchup for dinner on his couch. With bad breath.

I got up and checked out his video tapes. They were lined against the wall on the floor, on either side of his balcony door. Only a few of them were labelled. Exactly the kind of project Amy would totally get into. She liked organizing other people's stuff. She'd find the idea of possessing tapes of old baseball games to be utterly preposterous, but give her a marker and some labels and she'd be all over them. That was the place where her world and Ron's met. And that's where I lived: on the borderland, where the boundaries were a little obscure. I'd been passing back and forth between the two sides for as long as I could remember, never feeling completely at home in one, but missing it the moment I entered the other. I had always believed a time would come when I would be forced to choose. But what if I didn't actually have to?

I pulled out my phone and fired a text off to Amy. *Is tonight a trying night?*

I stepped outside to smoke. Ron's balcony was in the back of his building with a view of the alley. Anthony was three storeys below, looking content, sitting on an abandoned, decrepit mattress, a joint squeezed between his thumb and forefinger. I backed off the balcony, back into Ron's living room, my cigarette held between my lips. Ron's toilet flushed. The water ran in the sink for a second and the bathroom door opened. I put my index finger to my lips, signalling Ron to be quiet. I gestured at the balcony with my thumb, then pointed down with my finger. Ron crept outside and peered down. He came back inside, smiling.

"Anthony."

"Yeah."

"Poor you."

"He's a talker."

I followed Ron into his little kitchen. He opened a cupboard. He removed four drinking glasses, one by one, and placed them on the counter. From his fridge, he pulled out a red Tupperware pitcher, and poured red juice into the glasses until the pitcher was empty. I smoked and watched him rinse the pitcher before filling it to the brim with water. "You're considerate."

"I'm a nice guy. What can I say?"

My phone vibrated. I checked Amy's reply. *No but what the heck.* Another text arrived from her. *And thanks. Love you lots.*

I went out onto the balcony. Ron followed, steadying the pitcher of water with both of his hands. Down in the alley, Anthony was staring ahead at nothing, no doubt thoroughly buzzed. Ron turned his head and pressed his mouth against his shoulder, smothering laughter. I wondered if he could smell his own breath.

I wondered if maybe he was used to it.

When Ron got himself under control, he swung his arms back and then forward again, a rocking motion, and the water flung from the pitcher, flung into mid-air, then down in a cascade, showering Anthony. He screamed and shot up from the mattress. He spun once in place and wiped wildly at face, his hair, and his chest with his hands.

Ron turned to me and smiled. His Transitions were fully tinted. "That reminds me," he said. "I still owe you payback."

"See you tomorrow?"

"See you tomorrow."

# MERRY DU TERMINUS

The blind date was orchestrated by Leanne, the accountant at Bill's work who was curious but not nosy and talkative but not aggravating and lovely but not available. She said it like she really meant it when she said she couldn't believe Bill was still single, nearly four years after his divorce. Then, two days later, in the lunchroom, her microwave-warmed pasta primavera steaming in her Pyrex, Leanne told Bill about her friend Merry – "Merry, like 'Merry Christmas'" – who was also single.

"She plays the banjo."

"She's in a band?"

"No. She just plays the banjo. You should totally meet her. You never know."

Bill didn't know what to say so he said what Leanne said. "You never know."

"So you'll do it?"

"Do what?"

"Okay, you know the Nickels on Atwater?"

The waitress delivered Bill to a booth near the back of the restaurant where Merry was already seated. She wore an orange blouse that was adorned with purple, blue, and black floral designs. It crinkled loosely at the neckline and across her collarbone. The sleeves were rolled halfway up her forearms in a bunch. The thumb and forefinger of her right hand encircled the base of a drinking glass. Slivers of ice floated in the diluted remains of a Coke in the bottom of a glass, and a plastic straw leaned on the inside of its rim.

"I hope you haven't been waiting long," Bill offered.

"I just got here," Merry said. And ordered another Coke.

"And can I get something for you to drink?" the waitress asked Bill.

He was prepared for this question, but still paused before answering. He breathed through his nose. "Soda water. With lemon, please."


"So. It's Merry like 'Merry Christmas,' right?"

"Pretty weird, eh?"

"Not weird. Interesting."

"Interesting is polite for weird."

"No, it's careful for cool. I think it's cool."

Merry looked at her chicken brochette. She dabbed at her rice with her fork. Bill watched her and waited for her to say something. He thought she might be smiling. He waited nearly thirty seconds and then he cleared his throat.


His Adam and the Ants records clinched it. Merry said she didn't believe him. Bill thought she was pretending not to believe him. Either way, there was a pleasant quiver in Bill's belly. Merry said she would not believe him until he actually proved he owned two Adam and the Ants records. Just like that she was coming over to his apartment. Right after she finished her coffee and her slice of Rolo Cake.

He could barely touch his Chocolate Eruption.


When they got to Bill's apartment Merry hovered near the door and looked at the floor and yawned twice in quick succession. Bill undid his jacket but Merry kept hers buttoned. Bill sensed her unease. He didn't know where it came from. So suddenly. He felt guilty of a thing he had not done and would never even consider doing. In awkward solidarity, he zipped his jacket back up. "I'll go get the albums," he said. And left her leaning against the wall, between the door and his laminated *Trois Couleurs: Bleu* movie poster.

Around the corner, in his living room, Bill pulled *Kings of the Wild Frontier* and *Prince Charming* from one of his milk crates packed with records. Adam Ant on the album covers, the makeup, the clothes, the splendour. It wasn't funny anymore. He brought the records to Merry and showed them to her. She barely cracked a smile.

"Can I. Can I get you anything? Water? I think I have pineapple juice? If, um, you like that."

"Nothing. Thank you. Thank you but I better go."

"At least let me walk you to the metro. It's late."

On the walk they were quiet and then Bill cleared his throat. "I'm curious. What's the deal with Merry like 'Merry Christmas' anyway?"

"My mother told me she spelled it that way because she wanted me to be happy."

"Did it work?"

"I've been happy at times."

Bill offered to walk Merry all the way down to the metro platform. "It's nothing. I have a pass."

From the escalator, they saw a train leaving the station, going Merry's way. "It'll take forever for another one to come," she said. "You don't have to wait."

"I don't mind. And it won't take forever. But I could leave. If you want."

"No. Stay. If you want."

The station was nearly empty. They had their choice of seats. Merry sat first. Bill sat half in the seat next to Merry's and half in the next one over. "Which metro do you live at?"

"Côte-Vertu."

Bill held a fist to his mouth like he was holding a microphone and spoke in a robotic voice. "*Prochaine station: Côte-Vertu. Terminus.*"

Merry looked at the floor and laughed.

"You have a nice laugh, Merry. Merry du Terminus."


Bill rode with Merry up the Orange Line of the metro. She told him a story about a man who lived near her childhood home while she was growing up, a man who was blind. "People didn't know his name. We called him 'the blind man.'" There was a time when Merry's older brother and his friends had dropped their pants and mooned the blind man, right out on the sidewalk in front of the man's house. "This was my brother's way of testing him. To see if he was really blind." The blind man heard them giggling and had said, simply, *Hello, boys.* "So they all ran away."

Over the intercom in the metro, Côte-Vertu was announced as the next stop. Terminus.

Merry looked at her watch. "You're going to have to hurry. The metro's closing."

"I should be able to make it," Bill said.

When the metro pulled into the Côte-Vertu station, another one was already on the track opposite theirs. It filled all the windows on one side of their car. Merry looked at her watch again. "That's the last one for sure. You're going to have to run."

Bill stood up and positioned himself in front of the doors, holding the railing installed in the wall. He turned around to face Merry. "Thank you for a fun night." Bill staggered slightly as the metro braked.

"Maybe we can do it again some time?" The train came to a stop and the doors slid open.

"Go!" Merry said. She waved her hands in front of her chest like she was shooing mosquitoes. "Go, quick!"

Bill ran from the train and along the platform and up the stairs. The other train was chiming, signalling imminent departure. Bill ran across the corridor to the opposite stairs and flew down them. The doors closed and the train slowly began to move, gradually picking up speed, leaving Bill on the platform. Across the tracks, Merry looked at him with one hand held over her mouth.

"So, what happened with the blind man?"

"What?"

"You didn't get to finish your story. What ever happened with the blind man?"

"When my brother and his friends came around again, he told them if they didn't want their parents to hear about what shapely asses they had they'd better stay away from his property."

"So he wasn't blind?"

"Of course he was blind."

"Then how did he know they'd mooned him?"

"He had neighbours who looked out for him."

Bill shook his head and laughed. He turned and made his way up the stairs again.

Merry met him halfway across the corridor. "His name was Mr. Lockwood."

When they got to the triplex where Merry lived she invited Bill up. "Taxis run all night," he quipped, "so why not?"

Inside it was dark and it smelled faintly of chicken noodle soup. Merry flipped on a light switch near the front door. From where they stood Bill could see into the kitchen. There were empty plastic two-litre Coke bottles lined up on the counter, a half-dozen at least. There was a pile of dishes in the sink and another beside it. The cupboard doors beneath the sink were open, revealing an overflowing garbage can, onion peels and wet coffee grinds at the top. There were mugs and teacups and glasses in various places. There was a topless, empty can of baked beans on the counter next to the stove. All four burners held a pot or a pan; one held a pot in a pan. The floor was littered with toast crumbs, dust balls, and some grains of rice.

Merry led Bill past the kitchen and into the living room. There were more empty Coke bottles in there, on the floor and on the coffee table and under it. There was a flattened Ruffles All Dressed potato chip bag. Empty pizza boxes and a few Styrofoam takeout containers. An unruly stack of papers teetered on top of the television. Clothes, unfolded, sticking to each other, lay strewn all over the couch. Bill felt something brush against his leg and he stiffened. He looked down. A black and white cat meowed up at him. Bill looked at Merry. Merry looked at Bill. She stood there, frozen, her eyes squinted and her teeth clenched. Like she had just dropped something brittle and was too scared to look at it to see if it had broken.

Bill turned away from Merry and stepped forward, mindful of the cat. He made his way to the couch and sat down on it, on top of the clothes. He put his feet up on the coffee table, on top of a pizza box. He folded his arms and turned his head in Merry's direction.

"So. Leanne tells me you play the banjo?"

# PLAZA MONTCLAIR,
# EARLY SPRING

On a Sunday morning at the end of March, with the sun shining for the first time in what seemed like weeks, Marybeth sat on a bench in front of the dépanneur at Plaza Montclair, smoking a wine-tipped cigar she'd thieved from the pocket of her stepfather's jacket. Black cherry flavour. Her skull felt pleasantly squeezed.

There was a stillness about the strip mall. In the parking lot, so early in the morning, the lampposts outnumbered the cars. The few vehicles that did pull in parked over near the Provigo. Quick trips in and out for eggs and bread. A carton of milk. A tin of Maxwell House. And then gone again.

Marybeth plucked the woollen tea cosy she wore for a hat from her head and placed it on her lap. It was knitted in a checkerboard pattern of bright blue and white. There was a puffy pompom on top – white with bright blue speckles - and, on one side, a slit for a teapot spout. She'd been wearing it all winter; a joke from the bottom of a kitchen drawer, a joke her mother and stepfather failed to see the humour in. Her mother had asked her why she didn't just go ahead and wear oven mitts, too. Her stepfather said not to give her ideas.

Marybeth ran her fingers through her hair, encountering a few scattered knots. She tugged at them gently, loosening them, enjoying the resistance each knot offered. Once done, she clamped the cigar gently between her pursed lips and squinted for the smoke. With both hands, she fitted the tea cosy back on her head again, snug.

The sidewalk out in front of the stores was damp but now free of snow. So was the parking lot, except for the far edge that met with the top of a hill overlooking the autoroute. There, a line of snowbanks remained; sooty, twelve-foot piles from November through to February, a whole winter's worth of parking lot clearings. The snowbanks were melting, but sleepily; a series of slender rivulets flowed forth from their bases in dark, winding paths. Some of the streams merged near the boxy concrete pedestal of a lamppost. The collected water twisted slightly and washed down the squared holes of an adjacent manhole cover.

Marybeth smoked and watched the slow melt of snow. She listened to the autoroute hum beyond the snowbanks. She speculated vaguely on the genesis of rhythmic gymnastics. Her pleasant stupor was interrupted when, to her side, something caught her eye. From around the corner of the Provigo came Jono. Jono, Teenage Wino.

His hands plunged inside the pockets of his usual khaki trench coat, Jono sauntered in the direction of Marybeth's bench. His black boots were salt-stained, the laces undone. Jono's hair was black and his bangs were long and his lips were flat. His eyes were pretty. He had been absent after Christmas break, absent until early February. Rumours circulated at school. An ambulance in the night; a pumped stomach; rehab. The truth had proved far less glamorous. A divorce and a move to Repentigny with the dad but the dad had changed his mind and sent Jono back.

"Hey," Marybeth said.

"Hey," Jono said. He stood before her. "You got another one of those?"

Marybeth glanced at the smouldering cigar between her fingers. "It's my only one." She held it up in offering.

Jono smoked from the cigar. "Thanks," he said, barely exhaling. He stared past Marybeth, at the dépanneur's windowed storefront.

Then he looked down at her. "You don't happen to be eighteen, do you?"

"I'm not even seventeen. Why?"

"Doesn't matter." He wasn't looking at Marybeth anymore. He was looking at the dépanneur again. "Just asking. Just in case." He returned the cigar. He walked around Marybeth's bench and, after a few steps, entered the store.

Marybeth pivoted on the bench to look through the dépanneur window. The portly clerk behind the cash counter had a moustache and some amount of hair on his head. He wore a yellow uniform polo shirt with a name tag pinned to the breast. Jono arrived at the cash register with a bottle of wine. He placed it on the counter. Marybeth puffed on her cigar and watched Jono and the clerk have a discussion. Jono put some money on the counter. He pushed the bottle a little closer to the clerk. Then he pushed the money closer. The clerk crossed his arms and rested them on top of his gut. He shook his head. The two stared at each other. Jono reached into the pocket of his trench coat and drew a yellow water pistol. He pointed it at the clerk.

Marybeth got a stomach cramp.

The clerk did a sort of belly flop onto the counter, upsetting a little wicker basket of single-serving fudge squares. The wine bottle was knocked against the Tic Tac display. The clerk slapped the pistol from Jono's hand. Jono looked surprised. The clerk, lying on his stomach, rocked his hips from side to side and slithered backwards until his feet reached the floor behind the counter again. Marybeth found this equally funny and grotesque. The clerk turned to his right and scurried around the counter. Marybeth saw Jono, during the two or three seconds that the clerk's back was turned, snatch the wine bottle from where it lay on the counter and conceal it beneath his long coat. On Jono's side of the counter, the clerk smacked Jono's head once with his palm and once with the back of his hand. He pushed him toward the exit. The door flung open and Jono stumbled outside. Standing in the doorway, panting, the clerk announced he'd call the police if Jono ever set foot in his store again. Then he lumbered back inside.

"You are completely insane," Marybeth said.

"It's not like I was going to shop there my *whole* life."

"Want the rest?" Marybeth held out what remained of her cigar. Jono pinched it from her hand.

"I'm climbing those mountains."

They walked across the parking lot. Jono took a final haul from Marybeth's cigar and flicked it away. They began to scale one of the snowbanks. Jono slipped on the way up and, before she realized he was only pretending, Marybeth grabbed his wrist. Jono pulled her tea cosy down over her eyes and they laughed. They reached the top and descended a few steps down the other side. Jono removed his trench coat and laid it on the snow like a blanket. They sat on it.

Jono unscrewed the cap on the wine bottle and offered Marybeth the first drink. She took a sip. The wine was red and tart and it was still morning and it warmed her throat in a bitter kind of way. She handed the bottle back to Jono. He drank several uninterrupted swallows from it. When he stopped, he exhaled happily and wiped his lips with the back of his hand. A third of the wine was gone. He offered Marybeth another drink but she didn't want to have any more so she said, "Not right now." Jono tipped the bottle to his lips and drank again.

They looked at the autoroute and beyond it the roofs of houses in the lower part of town. Further to the south, far away on the horizon, stood the skyline of Montreal. The skyscrapers looked as small as toys. To the right, dwarfing the buildings, was Mount Royal. Saint Joseph's Oratory's domed roof stood out from the mountain's foliage. Marybeth extended her right arm before her and made a fist, except for her thumb, which she left pointing upward. She closed her left eye and positioned her thumb in such a way that the Oratory disappeared behind it.

"What are you doing?"

"Nothing," Marybeth dropped her arm to her side again.

"Come on, what is it?"

"It's nothing. Really. Forget it. It's just a thing. A thing my dad showed me when I was little."

"Well?"

Marybeth exhaled loudly, pretending to give in. "If you close one eye, you can hide the buildings behind your thumb."

"You can what?" Jono laughed.

"Just try it. You'll see."

Jono closed one eye. He held out his right arm and turned his thumb up. "Aha!" he exclaimed. He swivelled slowly from side to side. He laughed for each building that vanished behind his thumb.

Marybeth couldn't help but smile. The game had never failed to entertain children and anybody who was drunk.

"Whoa," Jono said suddenly. "Check it out." His voice was steeped in awe. "If you look with both eyes open, you can see the buildings *through your thumb*. It's like fucking X-ray vision!"

At Jono's repeated urging, and with more than a little reluctance, Marybeth tried this modification of the game. Indeed, keeping both eyes open produced the illusion of seeing right through her thumb. But it only made Marybeth feel slightly dizzy and vaguely annoyed.

After some minutes of silence and – on Jono's part – drinking, Jono got giggly. He declared it was time to get his spring tan. He removed his shirt and flung it in the snow. This was very funny to him. Marybeth got up to retrieve the shirt. When she came back, Jono was lying on his back, on his coat, both hands clasped behind his head. Except for his armpits, he was pretty much hairless and he was skinny. He had a birthmark near his right nipple that looked like a nose in profile.

"You're going to catch pneumonia." She attempted to cover him with his shirt but he pushed it aside. Then he craned his neck and tried to kiss her. Marybeth turned her face away. "You're drunk."

"You smell like a cigar."

Later, the bottle was empty. Shirtless, Jono dozed. Marybeth sat beside him in silence, her arms clasped around her drawn-up knees. She stared at the autoroute below. A blue minivan sped by. Marybeth turned her head to follow its progress. With every passing second, as it drove further and further away, the minivan grew smaller. Soon it was tiny and soon Marybeth couldn't see it at all. She imagined the people in the minivan: she pictured parents in the front seats and daughters in the back. They didn't know they had just disappeared.

Jono snorted. He shifted slightly. Marybeth held the back of her hand to his upper arm. His skin was like ice. She sat Jono up and worked his shirt back on him. She took the tea cosy from her head and slipped it over his. He mumbled a bit and tried to kiss her again but gave up easily enough. Marybeth threaded Jono's arms into the arms of his trench coat. With some encouragement and some shaking, she convinced him to stand. Taking his arm, she guided him delicately over the hill of snow and down the other side again. He stumbled a few paces into the parking lot and he wanted to rest. She steered him to the concrete base of the lamppost near the manhole. There Jono vomited. He made horrible sounds. Marybeth tried not to look but she saw some of it. It went on for a long time.

Then, she led Jono to the sidewalk in front of the stores. She took him to a bench near the Provigo, the furthest bench from the dépanneur, and helped him lie down on it. He went right to sleep. Marybeth reached for Jono's head but stopped herself. Asleep on a bench, wearing a tea cosy for a hat, Jono looked destitute and warm.

Marybeth rummaged through the pockets of Jono's trench coat. She found his phone. She bent forward and angled her head next to

Jono's, where the scent of alcohol was heavy. Holding her breath and holding the phone aloft, she took a picture of herself with the sleeping Jono.

She straightened and examined the result on his phone's screen. Her own smile stunned her. How genuinely happy she looked.

She set the picture as Jono's home screen image, slipped the phone back into his pocket, and left him sleeping on the bench.

Marybeth walked out of the strip mall parking lot. She turned in the direction of the overpass that connected the upper and lower parts of town. Halfway across, she stopped. She leaned against the ledge overlooking the autoroute and rested her arms on the concrete slab. The cars coming towards her grew larger until they disappeared loudly and abruptly beneath the overpass. Cars going away became smaller and, like the blue minivan, gradually vanished.

A white Jeep was driving away from her. Marybeth focused on it. She imagined what might be seen in its rear-view mirror.

Now it was she who was growing smaller.

So was the overpass. The strip mall, too. Soon the entire town of Montclair, with Marybeth somewhere within it, faded completely from view.

# ACKNOWLEDGEMENTS

Some of these stories have appeared previously in slightly different form. I thank the editors of these publications for their guidance: "Salut King Kong" in *Salut King Kong: New English Writing from Quebec*, edited by Elise Moser (Véhicule Press, 2014); "What Have You Done?" in *The Puritan*; "The Blind Man's House" in *ELQ/Exile: The Literary Quarterly*; "Spring Training" in *Geist*; "My Uncle, My Barbecue Chicken Deliveryman" in *CVC8 – Carter V. Cooper Short Fiction Anthology Series, Book Eight* (Exile Editions, 2019); "Little Brother, Remember the Christmas?" in *Rover*; "The Dad Was Drinking," "Something Important and Delicate," "Body Noises with the Door Open," "Merry du Terminus," and "Plaza Montclair, Early Spring" in *carte blanche*.

I thank the Canada Council for the Arts for the support it provided me to write this book.

Janet Black, KerryAnn Cochrane, Karen Smock, Gavin Twedily, and Elizabeth Ulin read early versions of several of these stories. I thank them profusely for their thoughtful feedback and encouragement, and for the community our workshops provide.

I am grateful to Barry Callaghan and Michael Callaghan, Editor-in-chief and Publisher of Exile Editions, for their faith and for their unshakable dedication. For his sharp and discerning editorial eye, thank you Randall Perry.

Marc Tessier read these stories and proceeded to design this book's beautiful cover. His superb talent and generous spirit allowed him to see, and make, what until then had only been a feeling.

For being the first (and right) person that I ever showed any of my fiction to, and for over thirty years of cherished friendship, thank you David Hansen-Miller.

To my dear friends who grew up with me in the suburbs of Montreal, and who still make me laugh today the way they did when I was sixteen, I thank you and raise a *fût* in your honour.

The words and music of Rush have inspired, comforted, and kept me company since I first heard them when I was twelve. With the works of Geddy Lee, Alex Lifeson, and Neil Peart at hand, this dreamer/misfit was never truly *so alone*.

My family is my haven, my biggest fans, and the greatest people I've ever known. So much love to Lynn, Cate, and Anika.